The Case of the Missing Bridegroom

A collection of short stories.

Romance
Mystery
Historical
Humour

by

Dawn Harris

ISBN-13: 978-1523913558
ISBN-10: 152391355X

To Susan
With thanks for all her support. And
for reading every humorous poem,
article, short story and book I have
ever had published.

Dawn Harris was born in Gosport, Hampshire, but now lives in North Yorkshire. She is married with three grown up children and two grandchildren. For more information see:-

www.dawnharris.co.uk

Contents

The Case of the Missing Bridegroom

I should have been working that Wednesday evening, keeping watch on a husband in a matrimonial case, but a personal crisis stopped me going anywhere. A crisis that threatened to wreck my whole future happiness. At ten o'clock that night, after my nerves had been cut to shreds and barbecued, I finally rang Detective Inspector Ricardo Smith's number.

Ricardo was my ex-boss. A genial, generous-hearted, forty-something celebrated pen wrecker, pink marshmallow popper, and the finest copper I knew. 'Carey, love,' he boomed pleasurably on hearing my voice. 'How's business?' I'd recently left the police force to become a Private Investigator. 'Clever idea, changing your surname. Carey Dent wouldn't catch the public eye, but Carey Warthog now----' An approving chuckle reached my ear. 'A different kind of pig, eh?' And he roared with laughter at his own joke.

'Ricardo,' I cut in tersely. 'I need your help. Neil's disappeared.'

'Disappeared?' he repeated, as if he'd misheard. His reaction was understandable; Neil and I were getting married on Saturday week.

I took a deep breath. 'Ricardo, Neil left work at five-thirty, and he still hasn't arrived home.'

'Good God, is that all?' he chortled. 'I didn't know you had the poor devil on a leash already. Look --- he'll have bumped into an old friend and gone for a drink.'

'Not without calling me first. We always tell each other where we're going.'

Ricardo yawned. 'So this time he just forgot. Men do, you know.....'

'I've checked all our friends and the hospitals. If Neil's been attacked, he could be lying injured somewhere, or suffering from temporary amnesia, or----' my voice broke on a sob, for no-one knew the awful possibilities better than I did.

'Carey, love.' Ricardo's voice was kind, but firm. 'I can't start a full-scale search for a bloke who's a couple of hours late getting home. I'd be a laughing stock.'

My voice quivered. 'Please, Ricardo. I just know Neil's in some kind of danger, and I'm --- I'm frightened.' The last word came out in a surprised whisper because I don't normally scare easily.

He heaved a long sigh. 'All right. I'll pass the word. Unofficially. OK?'

Thanking him, I then checked out Neil's usual ten minute walk from our flat to his office, still neglecting my Wednesday evening matrimonial surveillance. The kind of work that helped to pay the bills since I'd become, *Carey Warthog, Private Investigator. No job too small.* And they don't come any smaller than the Eccles case.

Mrs. Eccles, sharp-featured, black hair, gold-digger eyes, had steamed into my office, slammed the door behind her and, shaking her index finger at me aggressively, demanded, 'I want you to get me the name of the woman my Darren spends Wednesday evenings with while I'm at bingo.'

I learned from routine questioning that Mr and Mrs. Eccles were both thirty-five, had been married seven years, and had no children. Darren, recently made redundant from Safety First, a local security systems firm, had used his redundancy money to start his own removals business. Apparently, he had no hobbies.

'He swore blind he watched telly every Wednesday,' Mrs. Eccles raged. 'But, last week, I forgot my purse, and when I nipped back home to get it, the house was empty.'

'Perhaps he'd just popped out for a minute.'

She gave a derisive snort. 'Not him. I watched the house from the corner cafe, and he turned up shortly before I was due home. When I walked in, he pretended he'd been in all evening.' She leaned forward, her eyes cold and hard. 'All I want is her name, Ms Warthog. I know how to deal with her sort.'

I stormed into Ricardo's office early the following morning, close to blind panic, after a terrible night of fruitless searching for Neil. When he began asking me the usual "missing persons" questions, I banged my fist on his desk, causing a pink marshmallow to bounce right out of the bag. (He always had one within reach.) Ricardo popped it straight into his mouth as I exploded, 'We haven't had a row, Neil isn't worried about our marriage, and he can't run home to mother. Both his parents are dead.'

'I have to ask,' Ricardo murmured softly. 'You know that.' He speared several white marshmallows onto a pen like a kebab, and offered them to me. Ricardo only ever eats the pink ones. He says they help him to think. 'Last question. Fill me in on Neil's past. Friends before he moved here --- that kind of thing.'

I'd met Neil a year earlier, when he settled in Suffolk after working his way around the world. He had no family. In surprise I admitted, 'I don't think he's ever mentioned anyone.'

The telephone on his desk rang and Ricardo picked up the receiver. 'Yes?' His eyes gleamed. 'Brownings, you say? Yes, of course I know it. Industrial estate. Garden implements. When?' I watched him write *twenty-sixth* on the pad. Today was the twentieth. Grinning broadly, he mouthed at me, 'tip-off.' And said into the mouthpiece, 'Good work, Grant.' Detective Constable Tom Grant's informants were reliable, and no-one was more skilled than Ricardo at nabbing villains in the middle of a robbery.

Ricardo was still talking. 'What other business?'

I groaned. If only he'd stop nattering and find Neil.

'Oh, that,' Ricardo said, and listened, before glancing across at me, his expression suddenly unreadable. 'I see,' he murmured, and replaced the receiver so slowly it made my heart thump with fear. When he began to twist a pen absently with his fingers, my mouth dried up. I could write a thesis on his pen language. This particular habit meant he had bad news to break.

'Look, don't bother to wrap it up, Ricardo,' I whispered. 'I can take it, whatever it is. Just tell me.'

His eyes were full of compassion. 'Tom Grant says Neil was seen with a pretty young woman at five-thirty yesterday.'

'Where?'

'Outside Neil's office. Then they walked off down the alley together.' The alley was the only way out to the main road.

'I don't believe it was him,' I burst out.

'The person who saw Neil works in the office next door. He didn't know the woman.' I stared at him, unable to speak. 'I'm sorry, Carey. But better to find out now, than later.'

Ricardo insisted on driving me home, but he didn't stay. I refused to believe Neil had gone off with another woman ten days before our wedding. How could it be possible? He wasn't that kind of man, and besides, we were so happy together. I checked Neil's clothes, and our joint bank account, but nothing was missing. It was then I remembered the photograph album. This contained the only pictures he had of his parents, who had been killed in an accident when he was six. The album was his most treasured possession and the one thing he'd never, ever, leave behind. Running into the bedroom I feverishly pulled open the drawer where the album was usually kept. It was empty.

There were four rooms in our top floor flat, and I turned them all upside down. But the album had gone. I gazed unseeingly at the bedroom wall, thinking the unthinkable. Just then, the telephone rang and a familiar voice demanded, 'Well, have you got that woman's name yet?'

'Oh, it's you, Mrs. Eccles.' And I told her what I'd found out. 'Your Darren doesn't have another woman. He plays cards with friends in a small hired room at the Pig and Whistle.'

Mrs. Eccles' voice blasted into my ear. 'Last night my Darren came home with scarlet lipstick on his handkerchief and some female's hairs on his sweater. He didn't get them playing cards at no Pig and Whistle.'

'Woman's hairs?' I was taken aback. 'Are you *sure*?'

'Bleached, they were.' Angrily she sneered, 'You haven't been doing your job properly, have you?'

I sank onto the bed. 'I couldn't follow him last night. I was – er – indisposed, and....'

'Indisposed!' she screeched. 'Look, I'm not paying good money for you to be ill, Ms Warthog. What was wrong with you?' And she sniggered. 'Swine fever?' Her voice rose to a shriek. 'Well, I'll just have to find his fancy piece myself, won't I? Don't send a bill, because I won't pay it.' And with that final instruction she slammed down the phone.

Numbed and bewildered, I stumbled through the next few days, not knowing what to believe about Neil. Ricardo called frequently, mostly talking shop, and I reciprocated with the tale of Mrs. Eccles and her Darren. Well, if I wasn't being paid, it was hardly confidential, was it. But, when Ricardo began discussing his plans for the twenty-sixth, the day of the expected robbery at Brownings Garden Implements, I reminded him, 'You shouldn't be telling me all this. I'm not your Detective Sergeant now.'

'Got to talk about something, Carey.' Grabbing a stray pen, he bent it to breaking point. 'That stricken look in your eyes doesn't get any easier to take.'

On the twenty-sixth, Ricardo popped by, ebullient as ever. 'Everything's set up at Brownings for tonight. We're going to catch those blighters red-handed.'

I thought of him that evening, as I drove home in slow moving traffic. I had absolutely no doubt he'd nab those villains. A few minutes later, I was approaching a roundabout when I spotted Mrs. Eccles in the next lane. She didn't see me --- her eyes were fixed on Darren's green removals van which, as I then saw, was in her lane, about thirty yards ahead of her. That was when I remembered – it was Wednesday. Her bingo night.

Well, Darren couldn't be going to the Pig and Whistle, where the landlord said Darren and his mates had met every Wednesday for months, because that lay in the opposite direction. He must be visiting the scarlet lipstick and bleached hair instead. I couldn't help smiling. Clearly, Darren was about to get his comeuppance, without any help from me.

The lane Mrs. Eccles was in came to a total standstill, while mine moved slowly forward. As I went past Darren I glanced across at him, and saw he wasn't alone. What's more, one of his companions was a woman. A blonde. No wonder Mrs. Eccles was itching to get her hands on him!

A small gap between me and the car following, enabled Darren to force his way in right behind me. He followed me round the roundabout, and to my surprise, he took the exit signposted Marsh End, a narrow lane leading to a small village and a large country house, Marsh End Hall.

There was no sign of Mrs. Eccles, and on impulse, I circled the roundabout again, and saw her drive straight past the Marsh End exit. Traffic had prevented her seeing which road he took, and she wouldn't have expected it to be that one. Few cars used that road, and as I drove down it, there wasn't another vehicle in sight. Frankly, Darren's choice of destination mystified me. There wasn't a pub in Marsh End, and the people who owned the Hall were hardly.....

Gasping, I screeched to a halt, as I remembered who owned Marsh End Hall. Suddenly I felt as if I'd been sitting in a pitch-black room for the past week and someone had just switched on the light. At first, I was puzzled by what it revealed. But it quickly became crystal clear. The identity of the owners of Marsh End Hall made sense of everything else. Grabbing my mobile, I called Ricardo, and when he answered, I told him, 'You're at the wrong place.'

'I'm at Brownings on the industrial estate,' he hissed. 'How can that be the wrong place?'

So I told him how. The ensuing silence was broken only by an inarticulate splutter. I pointed out that the antiques and paintings owned by Mr. and Mrs. Browning at Marsh End Hall were far more valuable than the garden implements Browning & Co made.

Shortly before I left the police, I'd advised the Brownings on security, and I informed Ricardo, 'Mr. and Mrs. Browning always visit their son in Australia at this time of the year. So the house is empty, and the couple who look after it live in the village.'

I heard the familiar rustle of a packet of marshmallows. He was thinking. 'You're barking up the wrong tree, Carey,' he announced, chewing. 'The Brownings have a high-class security system, installed by that local firm, Safety First.'

Grinning to myself I played my ace. 'According to Mrs. Eccles, Safety First was the firm Darren worked for before he went into the removals business.' A loud groan deafened my ear and I laughed. 'When you arrest them, find out where they're hiding Neil.'

Ricardo choked down the phone, 'Carey love, take my advice. Go and lie down for a bit.'

He clearly thought I'd flipped with the strain, so I explained my theory. 'Look, Darren and his gang have been meeting at the Pig and Whistle every Wednesday for months now. Not to play cards, as the landlord told me, but to plan the robbery. Only his wife thought he was having an affair, and when I started nosing around on her behalf, I reckon the landlord must have tipped Darren off. That left them with two choices. They had to stop me following Darren, or call off the robbery. Well, obviously the only way to stop me doing my job was to give me something far more worrying to think about. So when they discovered I was getting married they knew exactly what to do. Arrange for Neil to mysteriously disappear. Clever, don't you think? And it worked. I stopped following Darren.'

Ricardo said one very rude word and started his car. Shortly afterwards, he arrested Darren and his gang while they were loading various art treasures and paintings into the van. Thankfully, Darren wasn't a violent man. He'd deliberately waited until the Brownings were abroad before robbing them. And, yes, he was having an affair with the blonde woman, but she was also part of his gang. Masquerading as a plain clothes policewoman, she met Neil as he left work, and informed him I was in intensive care following an accident. Knowing he always walked to work, she tricked him into going with her by offering to drive him to the hospital.

A couple of men were sent to release Neil from the disused barn where he'd been kept, and as I waited with Ricardo in his office, he summed things up in his own inimitable manner.

'So Darren's plan would have succeeded, if it hadn't been for his wife's suspicious nature, and we'd have a major robbery on our hands.' And he offered me a marshmallow. Not speared on a pen for once, but straight from the bag.

'A pink one?' I queried, stunned; for there was no greater sacrifice.

'Just this once, Carey, love.' And he grinned. 'You deserve it.'

Neil was unharmed, and when I threw myself into his arms, he murmured, 'What took you so long, Miss Marple?'

I retorted with a question of my own. 'Where,' I demanded huskily, 'is your precious photograph album?'

He stared at me. 'In the attic, of course. I put it up there last week, for safe keeping while we're away on our honeymoon.'

Days to Remember

I work in a florist's most mornings, and I was just making up an order when my daughter rang me. 'Can you manage lunch today? My treat. I have something to tell you.' She giggled. 'It's a day to remember, Mum.'

This last remark, according to my family, is something I always say on momentous occasions. And I'm never allowed to forget it. But Pippa sounded so happy, I let her have her little joke and merely smiled at her attempt to make her news sound mysterious. For I knew perfectly well what it was, of course.

Pippa and her husband, Peter, both vets at a local practice, lived in Peter's old, cramped flat and had been searching for their dream home for months. From the excitement in Pippa's voice, it was obvious that they'd finally found it.

At lunchtime, eager to hear all the details, I was walking through the high street to our favourite restaurant, when I was stopped by a young market researcher. 'Thank heavens,' he said gratefully, 'a woman under forty at last.' And, placing his hands together as if in prayer, he begged, 'You will help me, won't you? Five minutes, that's all it takes.' He lowered his voice. 'Please. The town's been full of nothing but grannies all morning.'

Laughing, I agreed. Well, what woman doesn't enjoy a spot of flattery! If he thought I was under forty, who was I to argue? He hadn't asked my age, so I hadn't lied. Anyway, I've always looked younger than my years. I work hard at preserving those looks. My hair is always the correct shade of auburn, and workouts at the gym keep my figure trim and willowy. I'm not going to ruin it by admitting how old I really am. OK, so I'm a touch sensitive about ageing. Show me a woman who isn't.

The questions took exactly five minutes, as the charming young man had promised, and I went on my way smiling, thinking how my husband would laugh when I told him about the encounter. Jon says a young-looking wife is good for his morale and he finds it very amusing that most people assume he's a good deal older than me. He's currently on a business trip to Japan. But, thankfully, such trips end for good in six months, when his company will merge with another. Jon, like some other employees in their late fifties, is taking early retirement. He's lucky to be able to do so, we know, and fortunately, we'll have enough to live on. Frankly, we can hardly wait. No more awful partings, no more being tied down. At last we'll be free to do whatever we like. We haven't made any firm plans yet, but one thing we are certain of is that we're going to have a ball.

Pippa was already seated at a table in the restaurant when I arrived, and after we'd ordered, I asked, 'So, what's this important news?'

Her eyes gleamed. 'I meant to wait until Dad came home so that I could tell you together, but it's no good. I can't keep it to myself any longer.' There was no mistaking the joy in her voice. 'Can't you guess? I'm going to have a baby.'

I'd just taken a sip of my drink and I choked badly. Pippa leapt up and slapped my back. 'Are you all right?'

When I managed to croak a yes, she looked at me anxiously. 'You are pleased, aren't you?'

I stood up and hugged her. 'Of course I am, darling. It's simply wonderful news. I'm surprised, that's all.' Pippa had known Peter for two years, and been married for just a few months. 'I thought you'd want to concentrate on your career for a few more years yet.' She had wanted to be a vet since she was five, and she'd worked hard to achieve it. Passing her finals had been a day worth remembering. Jon and I were immensely proud of her.

'We reckon we've timed the baby perfectly, Mum.' Chuckling, she cut into her salmon steak. 'Besides, on my next birthday I'll be th-----'

'Sssh,' I broke in hurriedly. 'Someone might hear you.' The restaurant was packed.

Pippa laughed. 'I don't mind people knowing how old I am.'

'Well, I mind,' I hissed, leaning across the table. Pippa, having inherited my youthful looks, was often taken for a teenager but, as I quickly pointed out, there was an obvious knock-on effect in revealing her true age. 'Just think how old that must make me.'

That made her giggle. 'You're not old, Mum. You're only----'

'Yes, yes,' I cut in hastily, glaring at her. 'There's no need to say it out loud.'

'Your secret's safe with me.' Pippa grinned. 'Anyway, all my friends think you look young enough to be my sister.'

'Really?' I purred. Now that was more like it.

My daughter's eyes danced with mischief. 'Do I detect a touch of vanity there, Mother? Don't worry, you're certain to be the most glamorous grandmother in town.'

'Grandmother!' I stared at her dumbfounded, and held on to the table for support.

'Well,' she giggled. 'You will be one quite soon, you know.'

That fact had somehow managed to escape me up until then and I staggered out of the restaurant in a state of shock. Jon would be thrilled about the baby and I knew I ought to be too. But I wasn't ready for this. I hadn't planned on becoming a grandmother for years yet.

I tried explaining how I felt to my sister, Marissa, during our weekly game of golf that afternoon. Marissa tends to speak her mind. 'What's your problem?' she asked in her forceful way.

I grimaced. 'It's just that I'm not ready to do --- well, you know, whatever it is grandmothers are supposed to do.'

Marissa sank a twenty foot putt. 'What?' she tittered. 'Like sitting in a rocking chair with your knitting?'

'Knitting?' I echoed in horror. 'I can't knit.'

'All grandmothers can knit,' Marissa smirked. 'It's expected.'

'It's all right for you,' I muttered enviously. 'Your kids are still at school.' She'd left motherhood late. 'You won't be a grandmother for ages yet.'

Grinning smugly, she murmured, 'I know.'

I burst out, 'You're really enjoying this, aren't you? Don't you see, it will make me sound so....so.....' Cringing, I forced myself to say it. '......so *old.*'

'Yes, I suppose it will,' she cackled. 'Still, you can hardly keep it secret, can you? You mustn't get so touchy, not now you have important decisions to make. For instance, do you want this child to call you Grandma or Granny?' she goaded, speaking slowly and savouring each word, as she lined up her next putt. 'Or Nana is quite popular, I believe.' I closed my eyes and shuddered. Did I really have to choose one of those? 'Mind you,' she went on, 'there are worse things to worry about.'

'Like what?' I was still reeling at the prospect of being called Granny in public.

'Will Pippa continue to work?'

'Of course. She loves her job.' Not that Pippa had mentioned it over lunch, but I had no doubts. I prepared to drive the ball off the seventh tee. 'Frankly, I don't see how that affects me.'

So Marissa told me how – choosing the precise moment I started to swing the club. 'Guess who she intends leaving the baby with ----Grandma.'

Stopping a drive in mid-swing is difficult, but I tried. The ball rocketed straight up into the treetops above me and I overbalanced, crash landing on my bottom. 'She wouldn't,' I said in a failing voice.

'Why not? Grandmas are much cheaper than childminders.' I recalled two of Pippa's friends saying those exact words and suddenly I felt rather faint. 'And you loved being a full-time mother.' It was true, I'd adored it, but I didn't want to do it again. Or be tied down, just when Jon and I would soon be free to do our own thing.

'When's the baby due?' Marissa asked.

'Soon after Jon stops work.'

'She's timed it perfectly then, hasn't she?'

I stared at her and gasped, 'That's exactly what she said over lunch.' And I hadn't guessed why. Stunned, I shook my head. 'I can't believe she expects it of us, Marissa. Not without consulting us first.'

'Can't you? Ask her than. Go on, ring her.'

I took out my mobile and glanced at my watch. Evening surgery started at four-thirty, and Pippa was always early. But as I waited for her to answer, I got to thinking. Pippa was my only child and I loved her dearly. How could I let her down if she really needed my help? Guilt made me hesitate. Maybe that's why the words came out wrong when she answered.

'Pippa, when you return to work after the birth, you'll need someone to look after the baby---'

'Mum, you're a Trojan!'

I gasped, floundering. 'I didn't mean----' But my voice was drowned out by the sudden sound of a seriously distressed animal.

Pippa said, 'Looks like an emergency, Mum. Talk to you later. I'll pop in after work.' I leaned back against the tree and closed my eyes.

Marissa sniffed. 'I was right, wasn't I?'

I nodded and explained what had happened to cut the call short. 'She thought I was offering.' I groaned. 'How can I tell her I wasn't?'

'Honestly, you are so chicken-hearted. It's simple enough, surely. Just tell her the truth.'

Back at my house, Marissa took pity on me at last and made the coffee. I picked up my favourite baby photograph of my daughter. 'When Pippa was born she had soft silken hair and Jon's eyes.'

'If you're going to get all slushy and sentimental, I'm off.'

'I only meant that no mother ever forgets the moment she held her baby for the first time.'

A breathtaking experience Pippa would soon enjoy. A day she would always remember. I hadn't thought of that until now. In fact, I hadn't thought of anything except how Pippa's baby would affect me. And in doing so, I'd lost sight of everything that really mattered. Including the baby itself. A new life. A child I would love and cherish. My grandchild. I felt a great surge of joy.

'Marissa,' I murmured in awe, 'do you realise that this baby will inherit some of my genes?'

'Don't worry,' she chuckled. 'Everyone has some cross to bear.'

I laughed, but I was beginning to see what this child was going to mean to me. In that moment, I saw my concern over how old I appeared to other people for what it was. A triviality. At least, in comparison to what I would gain. And it was time, I admitted to myself ruefully, to get my priorities right. I could even compromise about looking after the baby. After all, we'd always encouraged Pippa in her career, supporting her in every possible way. As I said to Marissa, 'I could do some childminding, if Jon agrees. Provided it's not full time. I mean, Pippa is used to us helping her.'

My sister gave a snort. 'Used to you making sacrifices, you mean.' Picking up her car keys, she stalked to the door. 'Put your foot down for once. That's my advice to you.'

Pippa breezed in after work, as promised, her eyes sparkling with happiness, and before she could speak, I began, 'About the baby----'

'Mum,' she interrupted, 'there's something I didn't say on the phone. Peter's sister has just become a registered childminder. And that's why we're starting a family now.'

I gaped at her, as the full meaning of her words sank in. 'You mean---- Peter's sister will look after your baby?'

'Yes.' Smiling, she put her hand on my arm. 'I knew you'd offer, but you've done enough for me. This is your time now, Mum. Yours and Dad's. Enjoy it.'

'Oh, we will,' I promised, hiding my relief.

When Jon rang later, I told him the wonderful news and he was every bit as thrilled as I'd expected. 'Life's full of new experiences, isn't it?' And he teased, 'Mind you, I never thought the day would come when I'd want to sleep with a grandmother.'

His familiar chuckle came down the line and my whole world righted itself. I laughed out loud. And I do believe I might have said something about it being a day to remember.

Psychic Serena

My friend Serena is a clairvoyant – a real, live professional fortune teller, with all the right clobber, from a crystal ball down to the mystic earrings. She's no fake, for even in her own life she never makes an important decision without consulting the crystal ball.

But if Serena's lifestyle is extraordinary, mine couldn't be more conventional. I'm a happy wife and mother, who does nothing more wacky than write the occasional poem. And I have no desire to know the future in advance. So how do I cope with Serena's psychic abilities? Easy. We have an agreement. Serena doesn't predict my future and I don't bore her with my poems. An arrangement that worked perfectly well for years, until the morning I received three postcards, all from different friends. Three fabulous pictures of exotic, faraway places.

When I called on Serena later that day, I showed her the postcards, grumbling, 'I never go anywhere exciting.' Outside, the fog which had engulfed us all week remained unrelentingly murky. Never had a holiday in the sun seemed more enticing. But, as my husband Jack and I have to watch our pennies, we holiday in Britain. Not that there's anything wrong in that. Britain is full of beautiful places, and we avoid those long queues at airports.

Serena said, 'You might go abroad next year, Keri----'

'Huh!' Pointing out of the window, I mocked, 'Did you see that pig flying past?'

She laughed. 'Poor Keri, you really are fed up, aren't you?' I was about to admit it was only the weather, that fog always gives me the blues, when her eyes began to dance. 'Wait here,' she ordered. And soon came back bearing her crystal ball.

'Oh no,' I protested, backing away. 'What about our agreement?'

'Just this once,' Serena coaxed with a winning smile. 'My sixth sense tells me your next holiday will be one you'll never forget.'

I grimaced. 'Look, Serena, the last time I let you predict my future, you swore blind I was about to meet a blond hunk currently making a killing in the money market. So what happened? On the way home I was accosted by a thief who nicked my purse.'

'Well, he was blond, wasn't he?' she retorted in injured tones. 'Anyway, I was only seventeen, and still learning how to interpret what I saw.' She placed the crystal ball on the table and appealed, 'Go on, you need cheering up. You can read me one of your poems to even things up.' Adding under her breath, 'As long as it's a short one.'

I had the feeling I was getting the rough end of the deal, but I capitulated. Anyway, I was itching to try out my latest poem on someone. It soon became clear, however, that Serena intended making the most of my moment of weakness. Having composed herself, she cackled outrageously, 'Cross my palm with silver then, dearie.'

I laughed, but her palm remained outstretched. 'You're not serious.'

'I am. I can't do it without.' As I well knew that was a downright lie, but I fished in my purse and thrust a five pence piece into her hand. She stared at it in disgust. 'Is that all you think I'm worth?'

'It's the only silver I possess.' And I peered closely into the crystal ball. 'Anyway, I can't see anything......'

'No, well you don't have the gift, do you?' she pointed out in supercilious tones. 'Now, be quiet. I need to concentrate.' I waited, but when she said, 'Ah, it's clearing,' I began to giggle.

'Shut up, Keri. How do you expect me to.....?' Then a triumphant smile crossed her face. 'I knew it. I can see an aeroplane!' She frowned. 'It's awfully fuzzy, I admit, but it is there. And yes.......there you are, on a beach, with waves rippling in the hot sun.' She grinned at me. 'Well, that settles it. Next year you're obviously going abroad.'

'Next year,' I scoffed, 'we'll be in Britain, as usual.'

She glared at me icily. 'Keri, everything I see in the crystal ball comes true. Honestly, it really does.' I didn't believe her, but it brightened up a dull, miserable day.

Most people are intrigued that I have a clairvoyant for a friend but, having known Serena since we were both at Green Lane Primary, it doesn't seem strange to me. Serena was psychic even at school, but after she correctly predicted my first boyfriend was about to dump me, I called a halt to her crystal gazing on my behalf. I didn't want to know in advance what was going to happen. Besides which, she occasionally misinterpreted what she saw. As my nicked purse proved.

Whenever I've asked her how she predicts the future, she shrugs. 'I don't know. I just see things.' Being a clairvoyant has drawbacks, however. For Serena, it's her love life that suffers. It takes a very special kind of man to cope with the insights that come with her profession.

'You'll meet the right fella one day,' I said, confidently making my own prediction. I was certain that some discerning man would look beyond the trappings of her profession and discover the warm-hearted Serena I knew, and of course, in time someone did. Mind you, even I didn't expect him to appear at the Christmas Fayre.

The Fayre was run in aid of local charities and, naturally, Serena gave her services free. I was her assistant, ushering people in and out, and putting the money in a safe place. Her last customer was tall, dark stranger. Not handsome but, as Serena often says, you can't have everything.

What he did have was brown hair, hugely expressive eyes, and an enormous grin. Crossing her palm with a tenner to help the charities, he asked in cheery unconcern, 'Now, my lovely, what does your crystal ball tell you about Gus Greenwood?'

Serena shot him a surprised look. Customers were usually nervous or curious, and often both. No-one bounced in without a care in the world and introduced themselves. 'Let's see,' she said, studying the crystal ball. Almost instantly she jumped back, gasping, 'Oh!' and put her hands over her cheeks, which had flushed a deep, deep crimson.

Gus leaned forward, his eyes gleaming eagerly. 'Tell me what you saw.' I stood there, agog with curiosity, for Serena never blushes. Her reaction could mean only one thing. She had seen not only Gus Greenwood's future, but her own, too.

She looked up into his eyes for what seemed an eternity, and when she finally dragged her gaze away, she was breathless. 'Er.....Keri ....why don't you......er......count the money or something.' She jerked her head towards the exit. 'I'll see to this gentleman.'

So I left. But with the greatest reluctance. Well, wouldn't you? I was dying to find out what Serena had seen in the crystal ball, but she sneakily left the Christmas Fayre without saying goodbye. And every time I rang her, the answer phone was on. In the end I pushed a note through her door, in the form of a poem.

Oh Serena, Serena! Wherefore art thou, Serena?
Where hast thou gone?
Verily, I believe thou hast forgotten thy oldest friend,
Whom thou left, high and dry, at the Fayre.
So, switch off thy wretched answer phone,
Call in for coffee, or else ring,
Unless thou wanteth another very bad poem.

Okay, so it doesn't rhyme or scan. When did I ever say my poems were any good? Anyway, tough measures were called for if I was to find out what was going on. And it did the trick too. The following day, Serena turned up at my house looking sheepish, yet with a glow about her I'd never seen before. 'I'm in love,' she burst out. 'Isn't it wonderful?' She sank back against the sofa cushions with a blissful sigh. 'It's Gus.'

I arched an eyebrow at her. 'You don't say.'

She laughed. 'Do you know, Keri, he only came to the Christmas Fayre to bring his mother. But then he saw me....'

'And he fell in love.'

She nodded and I demanded curiously, 'So, what did you see in that crystal ball that made you blush?'

She began to giggle. 'Wouldn't you like to know!'

Well, yes, frankly I would, but I could see she wasn't going to tell me. Instead, she talked about Gus non-stop for the best part of an hour, telling me why he was the most wonderful guy on earth.

Finally, she asked what I'd been doing, and I told her, 'Jack and I have booked our holiday.'

'Oh good. Where? Majorca? Barbados?'

Chuckling, I shook my head. 'Devon.'

'Devon?' she echoed in disbelief. 'Keri, I definitely saw an aircraft and the sun rippling on the waves. Perhaps you'll win a holiday, or even come up on the lottery.'

Tongue-in-cheek, I pointed out, 'You mean, you don't know? You're the one with the crystal ball.....'

She sniffed. 'We'll soon see who's right.'

Jack and I didn't win a holiday or the lottery, naturally, but Serena was right about the sun and sea – and in a sense, about the aircraft too. Because on the last day of our holiday I dozed off in a sheltered, isolated bay, while Jack went for a walk along the cliffs. And I woke up to find the tide had swept in and I – a poor swimmer – was completely cut off, stranded, and in immediate danger of drowning.

When I related that experience to Serena, and how I was rescued, she remarked, 'Well, I did say you'd get sun, waves and a trip in an aircraft.'

I almost choked. 'May I point out that the words "air-sea rescue helicopter,"' I said, emphasising them frostily, 'never passed your lips. Even though I crossed your palm with silver.'

Grinning at me affectionately, she said, 'Well, what do you expect for a lousy 5p?'

She seemed sublimely happy with Gus, until one day she visited me in a state of panic. 'Gus wants me to marry him,' she wailed.

I stared at her. 'For heaven's sake, what's your problem? You're nuts about each other.'

'Yes, but....' and her voice lowered to a whisper. 'It's the crystal ball. I can't see my own future any more. Not since the day Gus and I met. I'm scared, Keri. How can I marry Gus when I don't know whether we'll be happy?'

I laughed so much I could barely speak. 'Join the club. How do you think we mere mortals manage?'

She shuddered. 'I can't imagine.' Wistfully, she murmured, 'Gus is everything I've ever dreamed of.'

'Then forget your wretched crystal ball. Follow your own instincts for once.'

In the end she took my advice and hasn't looked back since. Or, come to that, into the future.

The Reluctant Father

I guess I'm a bit of a male chauvinist. Not that I would ever admit it, of course. But the fact is, I truly believe women are better suited to changing nappies and cleaning up baby sick than men. Well, it comes naturally to them, doesn't it?

Now, don't get me wrong. I do my bit around the house. I'm a dab hand at washing up and dusting. And when Lori, my wife, came home with the baby, I was happy to vacuum and cook. But it was Lori who looked after the baby. Like I said, that's women's work. Mind you, I really did intend to take a more active part, only it didn't work out like that. And that's how the situation stayed, until fate stepped in.

When Lori wanted to go away for the weekend, I assumed her sister, our chief babysitter, would look after Jessica. 'Leave her with Sue?' Lori echoed incredulously, looking at me as if I'd suggested dumping her in the middle of the Sahara desert. 'Jessica is your daughter too, Gavin,' she went on, white-faced. 'You see so little of her, I thought you'd enjoy having her to yourself for a whole weekend.'

'And so I would, darling,' I agreed glibly. 'But I'm playing cricket all that weekend. And,' I continued, 'I can't let them all down, can I?'

Lori stared at me for a long time, looking almost – well, almost as if I'd struck her. I simply couldn't understand it. I thought I was being perfectly reasonable. I would never deliberately hurt Lori – I love her far too much. But there are times when I do wonder if I'll ever understand what goes on in a woman's mind.

Eventually, tight-lipped, she muttered, 'I see.' And swept past me to pick up the phone. I went into the kitchen, reckoning I'd better show willing in some department, and I'd almost finished the washing up when Lori joined me. 'Sue says she'd love to have Jessica,' she said quietly, as a single tear quivered on an eyelash before dropping onto her cheek.

Horrified, I scooped Lori into my arms and kissed her. I had to come up with some pretty convincing lies – and fast – if I was to remove that tragic, hurt expression from her eyes. I threw myself into the role with gusto. 'Look, darling, I'm sorry,' I said, 'but I'm not much good with babies. Lots of men aren't. I'm really terrified of doing the wrong thing.' Well, I couldn't tell her the truth, could I? Jessica is six months old, a pretty baby with blonde curls and blue eyes. But I feel absolutely nothing for her. No love, no commitment. Nothing.

'I could teach you what to do, if you'd let me,' Lori said.

I frowned. 'I'd like that, but the trouble is she's usually asleep by the time I get home.' Then I weighed in with what I knew to be the clincher. 'There are the weekends, of course,' I mused doubtfully. 'Maybe if I cut down on my sporting.....'

"You'll do no such thing, Gavin,' Lori protested, outraged. 'You work so hard all week, you deserve to relax at weekends. Anyway, it's what we agreed before Jessica was born. I wanted to stay home with our children until they went to school, and you wanted to keep up your football and cricket.'

'As long as you're happy with that,' I said.

Okay, so I'm a heel. I know it. I felt pretty bad, I can tell you. Especially with Lori being so supportive. She's totally unselfish, caring and loving, with a great sense of humour. She watches all my football and cricket matches, cheering me on and helping with the refreshments. And it's just great to have her there. She's the best wife a fella could have.

Lori's weekend away was a reunion of classmates from her old school. They were meeting in London on Saturday evening and, as we live in Devon, Lori decided to go by train. When she packed the night before, her eyes sparkled in such happy anticipation, I put my arms round her, murmured softly into her sweet-smelling hair, 'Lori, I want you to have a wonderful time.'

At that moment the phone rang. 'Will you answer it, Gavin?' she smiled. 'I've still got to sort out Jessica's clothes.'

Picking up the receiver I gave our number, and a familiar voice said, 'Gavin, it's Sue.' She sounded out of breath. 'Bad news, I'm afraid. I can't look after Jessica after all.....' I groaned out loud. 'Sorry, but I've sprained my ankle. It's so badly swollen I can't even stand.'

She sounded really distressed and I called Lori to the phone. They exchanged a few words, and then Lori said, in a voice trembling with disappointment, 'I'll have to cancel my trip, that's all. What else can I do?'

Now, male chauvinist I may be; heartless I am not. I knew how much Lori had looked forward to this weekend and I was determined she should have her treat. She deserved it. There was only one thing to do and I did it. I crossed the room, put my arm round her waist and gulped, 'I'll look after Jessica.'

Lori gazed up at me, eager with hope. 'Are you sure?' I swallowed hard and nodded. Tears misted her eyes as she told Sue the good news. I pulled out of the cricket match immediately for, as Lori pointed out, 'They'll need time to find a replacement.' Adding consolingly, 'It's only this once, Gavin.'

By the morning I was beginning to regret the impulse of the night before. I mean, what did I know about babies? It was true, work had stopped me seeing much of Jessica. I'd spent six weeks away on a course and, now I was the sole breadwinner, I worked harder than ever. True I'd bathed Jessica and changed her nappy occasionally, but I'd had no sleepless nights, as Lori had breast-fed the baby until recently. And when Jessica cries, it's always Lori who comforts and cuddles her, never me.

Lori had written out a huge list of instructions covering every eventuality. She looked up at me rather anxiously. 'You'll be all right, Gavin.' It wasn't quite a question.

'Of course I will,' I said. But, as Jessica and I waved goodbye at the station, terror filled every fibre of my being. Jessica's bottom lip quivered a little as I put her back in the car seat, almost as if she knew she was a huge disappointment to me. Poor little soul, I thought, it's not her fault she isn't a boy.

Everyone had expected Lori to produce a boy; no girl had been born into our family for a hundred years. Her arrival, which had thrilled my family, had left me devastated. A sport-loving son would have completed my happiness. I heaved a huge sigh. How differently I would have behaved with a son too. Proud, loving, interested. I would have done my bit, shared the responsibility. Does that make me feel guilty? Does the sun rise in the morning?

Jessica gazed uncertainly at me when I went into the feeding and changing routines, but I coped. The afternoon being sunny and mild, I took Jessica to watch the cricket match I should have been playing in. While the wives fussed over Jessica, my teammates came in with the heavy barracking. 'Lori's got you under her thumb at last, eh Gavin?' And, 'What colour's your apron then, dearie?' All the usual kind of stuff. But, as none of them had such a wonderful understanding wife as Lori, it was easy to laugh off.

Only another 24 hours, I thought, as I bathed and fed Jessica that evening. After her bath she smelt so good, I found myself unconsciously kissing the top of her head, just as Lori does. When I settled her down in her cot, she fixed her blue eyes trustingly on to mine. She reminded me so much of Lori that my heart lurched a little.

Lori rang a few minutes later, and I was able to report confidently, 'Everything's under control. No problems at all.'

And it remained that way until midnight, when Jessica suddenly began to cry. Not the half-hearted squawk I'd learned to associate with a momentary waking up, but a full-blooded yell. I dashed in to pick her up, and changed her, but it made no difference. I tried giving her a bottle, only for her to push it away angrily. I paced up and down, cuddling her as Lori did. Nothing worked. She just kept screaming.

After half an hour, I was desperate. And very, very scared. Even though it was nearly one in the morning, I rang Sue, pleading with her to help me. 'All right, Gavin,' she said calmly. 'Don't panic. First of all, take her temperature.'

I followed her instructions and reported, 'It's normal.'

'Well, that's good. Now, tell me what she's doing, apart from crying.'

'She's stuffing her fist into her mouth and dribbling.'

'Ah,' cried Sue in triumph. 'There's your answer. She's teething.'

I was immensely relived. 'What should I do?'

'Frankly, Gavin, not having kids of my own, I don't know.'

'I wish you were here, Sue,' I groaned with heartfelt longing.

She hesitated. 'Sorry, Gavin, but I still can't stand up. Look, what Jessica needs more than anything is plenty of love. You can give her that, can't you?'

'Yes. Sure,' I mumbled. I put the phone down and remembering Lori's instructions, I grabbed them. Jessica had no teeth yet and Lori hadn't covered the subject. I was on my own.

Two hours later I was still pacing. Nothing seemed to comfort Jessica. Sometimes she yelled, sometimes she simply grizzled with her fingers in her mouth. I took her temperature again. It was normal.

All sorts of terrible possibilities kept looming in my mind. What if she wasn't teething? Did all lethal illnesses raise the temperature? I examined her for spots. Nothing. All the time one horrific thought hammered relentlessly in my mind. How would I ever face Lori if I let anything happen to our baby? Lori trusted me. She didn't know I felt nothing for Jessica. Or did she? Sometimes, when I held Jessica, I caught Lori watching me with an expression I couldn't quite fathom out.

If only I'd taken more interest in our child, I might have known what to do. I thought of the excuses I'd made not to get involved. Work, sporting commitments, odd jobs around the house. Anything. All put before Jessica, simply because she was a girl.

I had no idea it was possible to feel so scared about the safety of a child. But then, never before had my daughter been totally reliant on me for her wellbeing. Whenever I'd held Jessica, Lori had always been there ready to take over. Had Lori felt like this when I had been away on that course?

I broke into a sweat. I saw now that babies brought worries and responsibilities, and I had let Lori shoulder them all. Alone.

Even though we were equally responsible for Jessica being in the world. I'd let them down, and I felt deeply ashamed.

Around three in the morning, exhausted, I sank onto the sofa with Jessica on my stomach. After a few whimpers, she finally slept. The softness of her warm body against mine made me feel extraordinarily good.

The next thing I knew it was 9a.m., and Jessica was wriggling around. My left arm, which held her safe, was completely numb. I moved slightly and she woke up properly. One of her cheeks was still bright red. 'Poor love,' I murmured and kissed her soft blond hair.

She looked into my eyes and beamed. Then she said, as clear as could be, 'Da-da.' A sense of euphoric wonder ran through me, quickly followed by a tremendous guilt. No father deserved that accolade less than I did. Nevertheless, I rang Sue and related the exciting news.

'That's early,' she exclaimed. 'Lori said that wouldn't happen for another month at least.'

'Jessica's first word and I was the one to hear it.'

'Yes,' Sue remarked acidly. 'There's no justice is there?'

I realised then that I hadn't fooled Sue. She knew how I'd felt about Jessica. And if she knew....... I gulped and hurriedly changed the subject. 'How's the ankle?'

'Agony,' she declared.

As I gave Jessica her bottle, her hand curled round my finger. The expression of sheer bliss on her face, and the trust in her eyes, made me catch my breath. And I did some serious thinking.

I thought of my own father, solid and reliable, always there when needed. He had been one of the most important influences in my life. As I could be to Jessica. If I chose to be. Perhaps she would be musical, or a dancer, maybe even a sportswoman. But, whatever she was, I knew now that I wanted to be a part of it. My daughter would not have a male chauvinist for a father.

Already I'd missed out on Jessica's first six months of babyhood, but it wasn't too late. I was lucky --- this weekend had provided me with a second chance.

When I went to pick Lori up that evening, I was astonished to see Sue bounding along the pavement, tennis racquet in hand. 'Jessica,' I said, as the truth dawned. 'Will you look at that? I have been well and truly conned by two scheming women.' And I thanked heaven for it.

The Assignation

Stuart knocked hesitantly on Christabel's bedroom door, his heart hammering wildly. For the thousandth time he checked the note she'd thrust into his hand earlier that evening. *My room, 11p.m. Bring your toothbrush.*

From the moment Christabel walked into the computer room that morning, she'd commanded total attention. A strikingly beautiful blue-eyed blonde, her perfect figure was enhanced by a smart business suit. She was the instructor in charge of the five day IT course to which Stuart's firm had sent him and nine other new employees.

'Teachers,' whispered Stuart's nearest neighbour, 'were never like that when I was at school.'

At the end of the first day, when they were all relaxing in the hotel bar, Christabel had blatantly handed Stuart the note, right in front of all the others – and with one smouldering glance, had left.

They were all pretty merry by this time, and the new Cardiff representative had read the note over Stuart's shoulder. 'You lucky dog!' he gasped in envious tones. Snatching the note from Stuart's hand, he'd passed it round, pronouncing, 'Old Stu here has hit the jackpot!'

Stuart's face flushed a bright red, a colour that did not go well with his ginger hair. 'It must be a joke,' he babbled. No woman with Christabel's looks had ever given him a second glance.

'Hardly!' mocked Phil, the Cheltenham representative. Being tall, distinguished and good looking, he had strongly fancied his own chances. 'If you're not up to it, I'm perfectly willing to deputise!'

Clearing the constriction in his throat, Stuart thought of Jeannie and the boys back in Inverness and muttered self-consciously, 'She obviously doesn't realise I'm married.'

'Don't be so dumb,' Phil burst out, with a scathing laugh. 'Of course she knows you're married. She had all our personal details on file.'

'Forget the little woman at home,' urged another colleague. 'It's not as if she'd ever know.'

'Besides, Christabel must be crying out for it,' Phil sneered. 'Saddled with a husband like hers.'

Puzzled, Stuart demanded, 'What do you mean?'

'Good God man, don't you know? He's been in hospital for months. Paralysed from the waist down after a skiing accident.'

'But --- that's dreadful,' Stuart said.

'Well, y –e –s..... And no,' Phil drawled with a smirk. 'His bad luck looks like being your good fortune.' Leaning back in his chair, he finished his glass of whisky in one go, and smacked his lips. 'The question is, Stuart old son – do you have the guts to accept her invitation?' Then he sniggered in a manner that left no-one in any doubt about his own opinion.

The sea of grinning faces stung Stuart into retorting, 'Of course, I'm going. What do you take me for? A wimp?'

When the ribald comments finally dried up, someone suggested a game of snooker, and Stuart escaped to his room. Before the business of Christabel's assignation, he had intended to spend a couple of hours going over what he'd learnt today. He hadn't used a computer for his work before; in fact he'd never bothered with them much at all. He liked to be outside, walking or playing sport. The others all seemed to know much more about IT than he did, but he simply had to master it; he'd be working from home in Inverness, with no colleagues within easy reach who could pop in and help him out.

Yet, how could he think of work with Christabel's note scorching a hole in his pocket? He thrust a hand through his thick sandy hair and studied himself in the mirror. What on earth did Christabel see in him? He was so ordinary. Average in every way; height, build, looks, with hazel eyes and good teeth. Jeannie said she'd fallen in love with his smile.

Jeannie. He tried to picture her bright, elfin face and slim, boyish figure, but couldn't. Panicking, he took her photo from his wallet and her loving grey eyes smiled trustingly back at him. Childhood sweethearts they had been, and married at twenty-one. Much too young; he saw that now. And here he was, thirty next year, with sons of seven and five. Too much responsibility too soon. Jeannie was the only girl-friend he'd ever had. He'd never sown any wild oats, and surely a man was entitled to one lapse. His colleagues were right, only a fool would pass up a chance like this.

When Christabel opened her bedroom door, Stuart stood awkwardly in the open doorway. He'd never been unfaithful to Jeannie. Yes, they had married young, but he'd loved her then, and he loved her now. The others had said Jeannie would never know about Christabel. But he would know, and he realised the moment Christabel opened the door that he didn't want to live with that.

Christabel smiled at him invitingly. 'Are you going to stand in the doorway all night?' She wore the same figure hugging dress she'd had on at dinner, and Stuart nervously fingered his collar. 'Yes......no....er, I mean....'

Striding purposefully towards him, Christabel removed the hand tightly clutching the door handle, shut the door and locked it. Stuart broke out into a sweat. 'Look ....I can't....I'm happily married.'

'Yes,' she agreed complacently. 'That's exactly why I chose you.'

'Ch—ose?' he choked, wide-eyed and trembling.

She nodded. 'Let me explain. I wangled my way into this job shortly after my husband had his accident.' She raised a questioning eyebrow. 'You do know about that, I suppose?'

'Yes,' he admitted in a hoarse whisper. 'I'm so sorry.'

She sat on the edge of her bed, absently smoothing the duvet cover. 'My husband's situation causes me certain.....um.....shall we say, difficulties.' Looking up, she fixed her eyes on his. 'I don't have to spell it out, do I?'

In a strangled voice he replied. 'No—oo, of course not.' It was true, then. Christabel was a raving nymphomaniac. The key was still in the lock; perhaps he could make a run for it.

'So on the first day of each course, I make an assignation with someone like you. Someone kind, generous and thoughtful. A man who understands my predicament. It's worked very well, so far.' Stuart opened his mouth, but no sound came out. 'No-one believes the truth,' she went on. 'That I love my husband and only took the job to be near the hospital. Luckily, I find that happily married men rarely want to cheat on their wives. We spend an hour together every evening, watching TV, and hey presto, the men who think I'm fair game leave me alone.'

Stunned, Stuart managed to gasp, 'But, how did you know I.........'

'Happiness and contentment show in the face,' she said gently. 'Now, which channel shall we watch?'

Eagerly he blurted out, 'Blow the telly. There's something else I'd much rather do.'

Christabel glanced up quickly and warned in icy tones, 'Now look.....'

'Please,' he begged. 'I desperately need some help with this wretched IT course.'

An Offer of Marriage

The two occupants of the luxurious chaise travelling back to London were unusually silent. Mrs Henrietta Wetton, the wealthy widow to whom the chaise belonged, was leaning back resting her eyes. While her young goddaughter, Miss Sophie Cunningham, whose willowy elegant beauty had taken London society by storm this season, was forcefully reminding herself that beggars can't be choosers.

She had come to London to find a suitable husband. And if an offer of marriage from an immensely likeable young man like Lord Duffield wasn't suitable, she didn't know what was. She had no right to feel miserable. And no right whatsoever to long, with every fibre of her being, that the offer had come from Adam. For Adam Wetton, the elder of her godmother's two sons, had made it mortifyingly plain that he had no intention of marrying her.

Despite her distress, Sophie suddenly began to giggle. For the large feather on her godmother's hat had slithered over the end of her nose, and was now wafting up and down in time with her breathing. Before her stay in London, Sophie had only ever communicated with her godmother by the occasional letter. Since her arrival, however, she had quickly become enormously fond of the rather indolent Mrs Wetton, whom she'd always known as Aunt Hetty.

Most of Sophie's life had been spent on the Continent, where her father's artistic talents had, unfortunately, remained largely unrecognised. Her parents had nine children to establish in the world and very little money with which to achieve it, thus the future of them all depended on Sophie making a good marriage. Aunt Hetty had put her situation in a nutshell.

'Your lack of fortune is a handicap, my dear, but you don't want for sense. Should a man of comfortable means make you an offer -- one whom you do not find repulsive, of course, then I need not tell you where your duty lies.'

Her aunt had chaperoned her on an endless round of balls, routs, assemblies, visits to museums, theatres and the opera; she had been presented at court, and met "Prinny," as Aunt Hetty called the corpulent Prince Regent. All of which they had both enjoyed enormously.

Now they were returning from a short visit to the country, where the party had included both Adam and Lord Duffield. A visit which had terminated in this morning's humiliating interview with Adam. The memory of which was so past bearing that tears filled her eyes and threatened to spill over. But she forced them back as Aunt Hetty opened her eyes, sat up straight, carefully adjusted her hat and glanced out of the window.

'Hounslow Heath,' she said with satisfaction. 'We'll be home in good time for dinner.' Observing the pinched look on Sophie's face, she asked solicitously, 'Is there anything wrong, my dear?'

Sophie raised a pair of desolate, misty eyes. 'Last night I received an offer from Lord Duffield.'

Aunt Hetty's heart sank. 'Did you accept?'

'I....I asked for time to consider the matter.'

'Quite right. Most proper.'

Duffield was a wealthy and universally liked young man, and Hetty believed he would make Sophie an excellent husband. It was just that, with her younger son already happily married, was it wrong to want the same for Adam? And if he wasn't in love with Sophie, then she was the Archbishop of Canterbury.

'I don't suppose Adam has....' she began tentatively. Sophie shook her head vigorously, not trusting herself to speak. For Adam had given her no choice now but to forget those expressive dark eyes, smooth aristocratic features and that disarming smile which made people forgive his impatient nature. 'Oh dear,' sighed Aunt Hetty. 'I did so hope that he'd forgotten all that other nonsense.'

Until this morning, Sophie hadn't known there was any nonsense to forget. Nor had she known why Adam had taken to avoiding her lately. When a small sob escaped her, Aunt

Hetty patted her hand. 'All is not yet lost, my dear. Besides, there is no doubt in my mind that you would be the perfect wife for my son.'

'But Aunt, if Adam doesn't wish to marry me.....'

'Of course he wishes to marry you. He just doesn't realise it yet! So we must use a little subterfuge, something to push him in the right direction.' Nevertheless she added prudently, 'Don't let Duffield off the hook yet ----- just in case.'

She had just begun to regale Sophie with the story of her own stormy courtship, when the chaise suddenly lurched to an abrupt halt. 'What on earth....' Aunt Hetty blurted out, just as the door was torn open to reveal a rough looking man with a scarf over the lower half of his face, pointing a pistol at them.

Aunt Hetty screamed and promptly fainted. But Sophie's steady gaze held a hint of steel and in a voice that barely trembled, she warned, 'Our escort is but a short distance behind...'

'Well, 'e ain't 'ere now, is 'e,' the ruffian sniggered. And rapidly removed Aunt Hetty's vast array of rings, bracelets, brooches and her valuable necklace.

Sophie's only adornment was a pretty locket, a much-treasured present from her father. She tried to cover it up, but the highwayman hissed, 'Give that 'ere, or I'll shoot.'

Adam, riding back to London alone, heard two shots ring out as he approached Hounslow Heath. Instantly spurring his horse into action, his heart almost stopped when he saw two inert figures on the ground by his mother's stationary chaise. For there was no mistaking Sophie's sky blue pelisse, which so enhanced the colour of her enchanting soft grey eyes.

She had been wearing it this morning when she had deliberately waylaid him on his way to the stables, remarking in her direct way, 'Mr Wetton, would you care to walk in our host's splendid walled garden before we leave?'

Startled, he bowed slightly and acquiesced, her nearness playing such havoc with his senses, he'd almost given way to the overwhelming urge to throw caution to the winds, crush her in her arms and kiss her in a decidedly thorough manner. Only the sure knowledge that he would deeply regret it later had stopped him.

He'd listened gravely as she told him of Duffield's offer and asked his advice. Adam understood her meaning perfectly. She was giving him his chance, and if he didn't take it, Sophie's circumstances would compel her to accept Duffield. He'd muttered hoarsely that Duffield was an excellent fellow, expecting her to then drop the subject. But Sophie was made of stronger stuff than that. Indeed, her bluntness had taken his breath away. With scarlet cheeks, she had whispered, 'Have.....have you never thought of marriage, Mr Wetton?'

'Once,' he admitted in a harsh, cynical voice. 'When I was twenty, I nearly eloped with the most beautiful, gazelle-like creature I'd ever set eyes on. Fortunately, our plans were discovered in time.'

'Fortunately?'

'She was sent to relatives in Scotland for six months. Sadly, I'd completely forgotten her in two.' A small gasp escaped Sophie's lips, and he commented with rueful irony, 'Exactly, Miss Cunningham. She is now the happy mother of several children, her figure has enlarged accordingly, and I really cannot imagine what I ever saw in her.'

Sophie met his eyes frankly. 'Undoubtedly a lucky escape.'

'Indeed it was.' Having reached the garden, he held the gate open for her. 'Unfortunately, my interest in any other woman has also been of a similar short duration.' His eyes darkened. 'As I obviously do not have the constancy essential for a happy marriage, I prefer to remain a bachelor.'

Sophie hesitated. She had already said far more than was proper, yet life without Adam was too bleak to contemplate. 'Forgive me, Mr Wetton, but these experiences you speak of--- perhaps you simply had not yet met the right person. Your brother, for instance, has been luckier in that respect, has he not?'

'My brother? Perhaps.' Adam shrugged. 'I'm thankful he has sons to whom I may safely leave my fortune, but his happy marriage is tempered by his being saddled with an intolerable collection of his wife's grasping relatives?' His lip curled with contempt. 'I can imagine nothing worse.....'

Sophie had never been more mortified. Her chin shot up in defiance, her eyes blazed with outraged fury, and in a voice that vibrated with barely controlled anger, she burst out, 'You have said quite enough, Mr Wetton.' And with a swirl of her skirts, she turned and swept abruptly back towards the house.

Adam gasped. How could he have forgotten Sophie's large and penniless family? Cursing his crass stupidity, he called after her, 'I didn't mean.....'

But it was too late. Sophie, too proud to let him see she was crying, refused to look back. Yet, if she had, all might have changed, for Adam's eyes were filled with a longing no woman could misunderstand.

Desperately, Adam tried to convince himself it was all for the best. In a few weeks, when his interest inevitably palled, she would thank him. Sophie deserved to be happy, and Duffield would never give her a moment's heartache or pain. Yet, unaccountably, that thought caused him to put such pressure on the riding crop in his hands that it snapped in half.

The whole of that disastrous episode flashed through Adam's mind as he rode hell for leather towards Sophie, who lay motionless on the ground with her head slumped on the coachman's chest.

Adam felt as if the world had come to an end. What a fool he'd been to imagine he could give Sophie up. He needed her as much as he needed air to breathe.

He caught sight of her blue bonnet, discarded by her side. If only she was alive, he would shower her with bonnets. Grey ones to match her eyes, chestnut concoctions for her hair, and pink for those lips he'd never kissed. He would grovel at her feet, settle money on her pesky family, and house them all if that would make her happy. If only she wasn't dead.....

Adam leapt off his horse and fell to his knees beside Sophie. Having ascertained, with unutterable relief, that she was still breathing, he murmured distractedly, 'Sophie, my darling girl.....' And continued to whisper endearments with the fervour of a man passionately and hopelessly in love. At the precise moment Sophie opened her eyes, a piercing scream emanated from the chaise. Mrs Wetton had come round.

'I must go to her,' Sophie insisted shakily and, despite Adam's protests, she stood up. 'I'm not injured, Mr Wetton,' she assured him, fingering her locket. 'I...I think I must have fainted.'

'Miss Cunningham,' Adam began, taking her hands in his, and looking at her in a manner that sent a delicious shiver up and down her spine, 'there is something of importance I wish to say to you....'

It took all of Sophie's iron will to remove his hands, to reproachfully remind him, 'Mr. Wetton, the coachman is still unconscious and requires a doctor at once. In grappling with the thief he collected a bullet in the shoulder. Another shot grazed his head.' And she added gently, 'Besides, your mother needs me.....'

Flushing slightly, Adam bowed. 'I beg your pardon. You are quite right, of course.'

He drove them home, and sent for his own doctor, who attended to the coachman and made him comfortable. The doctor then prescribed sleeping draughts for the two ladies, thus further thwarting Adam's urgent desire to speak to Sophie.

Unable to present himself at his mother's house again until morning, he spent half the night pacing up and down his bedchamber like a caged lion. He had to reach Sophie before she gave Duffield his answer. But what if she refused to see him? What if his thoughtless remark about her grasping relatives had put him beyond the pale?

Thus, it was a very impatient and tense Adam whom the butler ushered into the parlour where his mother was partaking of a leisurely, and solitary, breakfast. 'Where's Sophie,' he demanded, without ceremony.

Mrs Wetton put an agitated hand to her temple. 'Please Adam, do not shout. My nerves are still shot to pieces after yesterday.'

'I'm sorry, Mama, but I must see Sophie before she speaks to Duffield. She thinks I don't mean marriage and....'

'Why would she think that?' his mother queried artlessly, her nerves not preventing her from buttering a third piece of toast.

'I told her so,' he growled, and put his head in his hands. 'Mama, I have made a proper mull of it all.'

'So it would appear.' Her lips twitched, but she asked with commendable gravity, 'Am I to assume you have changed your mind?'

'Yes,' he replied fiercely. He stood looking out of the window at the busy street below, his hands clenched behind him. 'Mama, I thought my lack of constancy in love was a flaw in my character. That it would be the same with any woman, no matter how strong my initial feelings were. But when I thought she was dead,' his voice shook at the recollection, 'that was the leveller. I knew I simply couldn't live without her. She is so far above any woman I've ever known.'

He stopped, recognising the man now calmly walking down the front steps of the house. Adam swung round, his eyes flashing with anger. 'Duffield was here all the time. And you knew.....'

'He called to see how Sophie was after yesterday's adventure,' she responded impassively. 'I thought it wiser not to mention it in your present agitated state, in case you felt it necessary to run him through. However.....' She broke off as the door opened, and looking up, she smiled with pleasure. 'Ah, Sophie, my dear....'

Adam reached Sophie in three purposeful strides, caught her hands in his and threatened, 'If you have accepted that eminently suitable young man's proposal, I shall be forced to cut out his heart.'

Sophie gazed fearlessly into those dark smouldering eyes that she loved and gurgled with delight. 'How very fortunate then that I refused him. To save Lord Duffield from certain death, and you from the scaffold, all in one day is surely......' At this point, Adam took her hands in his, before crushing her into his arms and kissing her in a manner that prevented all speech for some considerable time.

With a satisfied smile on her lips, Hetty quietly left the room. She'd known what the outcome would be ever since Sophie had revealed Adam's reaction to finding her lying motionless with her head on the coachman's chest.

'The truth is,' Sophie had explained, her eyes alight with mischief, 'I was listening for the poor man's heartbeat. Thankfully it was very strong, so when I saw Adam riding towards us like a madman, I decided to try the kind of subterfuge you suggested. I simply shut my eyes, lay still and pretended I was, at the very least, unconscious.'

Women Like Us

I burst into my mother's house like a tornado. 'Mum, I've got to borrow-----'

'Do shut the door, Trish,' she urged as she greased a cake tin.

Slamming the door shut, I burst out, 'Mum, I've met him!'

'Met who, love?' she inquired absently, as she weighed out the flour.

'Your future son-in-law, of course.'

Her eyebrows shot up so fast they nearly hit the ceiling. Well, I was thirty-two years old, and she'd had a long wait.

My stepfather, hearing the noise, came in to greet me. 'Hello, freckle face,' he said affectionately, giving me a great big hug. 'So you've finally got yourself a man, eh? What did you use? Handcuffs?'

I laughed, but Mum leapt to my defence. 'Don't be so cruel, David. You know how difficult it is for women like us.'

By "women like us" Mum meant six foot tall freckle-faced redheads. Believe me, men do not fall in love with that kind of woman on sight. Just getting a date takes time, patience and cunning. Particularly cunning. It took Mum three months of careful scheming before my father discovered he couldn't live without her. And after she was widowed, David held out for a whole year. 'You see, I was older then,' Mum explained, a touch of irony in her voice.

But I didn't have three months, let alone a year. I'd known Murray exactly two hours. And I had, perhaps, two or three weekends, if I played my cards right. I didn't have a moment to lose. I told them the little I knew about Murray, what I wanted to borrow, and why. 'You scheming little hussy,' David spluttered.

Mum laughed, but she understood better than anyone why I needed to use a little subterfuge. All right, so I was going to lie. I would have preferred not to, but it was the only way. 'Must fly,' I said. 'Wish me luck!'

Murray, a drop-dead gorgeous blond giant from Australia, had walked into our cake shop shortly before closing time. In fact, just as Felix, my business partner, was about to start knocking down a wall so that we could enlarge our highly successful venture. This weekend was the perfect time to get it done as Mrs. Young, who rented the flat above the shop, would be away tonight, returning tomorrow evening.

Felix was the one who made the scrumptious cakes, while I looked after the business side and did my bit serving the customers too. I liked meeting people.

Murray bought a coffee and walnut cake, and asked for some information. The moment I looked at him I could almost hear the wedding bells, but experience had taught me it wouldn't be the same for him. Somehow I had to find a way to stop him walking straight out of the shop and out of my life forever. David was right to call me a scheming little hussy. Well, it was the only way.

I gave Murray his change and asked what information he wanted, praying it wasn't just directions. Smiling, he explained, 'My family came from this town originally, and my great-aunt wants me to trace any relatives still living here.' Grinning at me across the counter, he spread his hands out in a gesture of helplessness. 'Only I haven't a clue where to start.'

'Well, actually,' I murmured, hardly able to believe my luck, 'I'm keen on family history myself.'

Felix, who was standing beside me, studying the plans for the extension, naturally heard every word. But I ignored his strangled choke, which came as a result of him having watched me bin a leaflet from the local family history society only the previous day, with the words, 'Trace my dead relatives? They must be joking. The live ones give me more than enough trouble!'

'Who are you looking for exactly?' I asked Murray.

'Well, the family name is Vestor----'

I blinked in surprise. Felix opened his mouth to speak, but I fixed him by skewering his foot to the floor with my stiletto heel. An action luckily hidden by the shop counter. I didn't want him blowing my chances of keeping Murray here. And while Felix was temporarily speechless, I took Murray over the road for a glass of wine, where we could talk in peace.

'I'm working in London at the moment,' Murray explained. 'My plan was to look up the Vestors in the phone book, pay them a visit, take photos, and send everything to my great-aunt. Get it all over and done with in one weekend.' He sipped his wine. 'Only there are no Vestors listed in the phone book.'

'Ah,' I murmured, feverishly wondering how to prevent him finding the answers he wanted, until he showed some sign of succumbing to my charms. I twisted my wine glass in my fingers. 'What do you actually know about the Vestors?'

'Only that when my great-grandfather emigrated to Australia at the start of the 20th century, his brother Jeremiah went to America. Jeremiah's plan was to make enough money to come home, buy a farm and marry his childhood sweetheart.' He thrust a hand through his gorgeous thick hair. 'My great-aunt doesn't know if he made it back, and I promised to find out.'

'In that case we'll start our search first thing tomorrow.'

'That's real kind of you, Trish.' He glanced out the window at the abbey, a magnificent Norman edifice, which was the usual reason tourists visited our small town. 'Where do we start? At the abbey?'

'No. You won't find anything in there,' I lied hurriedly. 'Better to look at the gravestones.' They wouldn't help him one bit.

'OK.' And he smiled at me, turning my knees to jelly. 'You're the boss.'

I hesitated. 'I was wondering --- would you like to come to a party tonight? I was going with Felix, only there'll be dancing, and he's – um – hurt his foot.' Felix hadn't wanted to go anyway.

'Sounds great.' His gorgeous grin made my heart turn right over. 'It beats sitting alone in my hotel room.'

Most things would. Ah well, it was a start. I left him then to make that hurried visit to Mum's, to borrow what I needed. After which I changed, collected Murray, and as we set off for the party, he told me, 'I managed a quick look in the abbey churchyard before I went back to the hotel.'

Forcing myself to stay calm, I asked, 'Did you go inside the abbey itself?'

Raising a surprised eyebrow, he protested, 'You said there was no point.'

'There isn't,' I stated in relief. 'Did you ---er --- find any interesting gravestones?'

He shook his head. 'But I did speak to a very nice lady. She was most helpful.'

'Oh yes? What did she say?'

'That there were a lot of other churchyards I could try.'

Later, dancing to *Lady in Red*, I asked Murray, 'How tall are you exactly?'

'Six foot, six and a half inches.'

I sighed. 'It's wonderful not to be looking over the top of a man's head.'

Chuckling, he said, 'It's great for me too. Most women don't even reach my shoulder.' And he rested his cheek cosily against mine.

Mum popped in early the following morning for a progress report, and casually remarked, 'Did you know a Vestor once owned Hill Farm?'

'But that's derelict now, isn't it?'

'True, but Murray doesn't know that,' she pointed out conspiratorially. 'It's in a glorious spot. Isolated too.' And she rolled her eyes at me.' Well, you can't afford to waste time, can you?'

So I drove Murray high into the hills. He accepted the derelict state of the Vestor farmhouse quite philosophically, commenting, 'It certainly suggests that Jeremiah came back from America. Now all we have to do is find his descendants.'

While he took a closer look at the farmhouse, I quickly disconnected the battery leads. Well, there was no point spending the day looking for his long-lost relatives. I knew where they were. And once Murray had that information, he'd made it perfectly clear he intended to leave town, never to return.

When the car refused to start, he eyed me roguishly. 'Have we run out of petrol?'

'Of course not,' I laughed innocently. 'Um --- do you know anything about cars?'

'Not a thing,' he responded cheerfully. 'Do you?'

I could strip down an engine faster than most, but I shook my head. 'Sorry.'

He leaned back in his seat, perfectly relaxed, hands behind his head. 'I suppose we'd better phone a garage.'

'Yes, I suppose so.' I searched my bag for my mobile, but it wasn't there because I'd deliberately left it at home. 'It's not here,' I said, pretending to be exasperated.

'And mine's back at the hotel.'

That *was* fortunate. 'Never mind. There's a garage at the next village. It's only five miles over the hills.' I glanced at him and he smiled, an unreadable expression in his eyes. 'Don't worry, it's easy walking.'

The sun shone from a clear blue sky, and we walked along chatting with the ease of old friends, with nothing to distract us from the beauty of the hills and patchwork of stone walls, except for the occasional sounds of birds and sheep. The longer I spent with Murray, the more convinced I was that this was the man I wanted to spend the rest of my life with.

At about half way we stopped to rest a while, and when I stretched out in the sun, he actually leaned over and kissed me lightly on the lips. Now that's what I call progress!

We arranged for the garage to pick up my car, had a late, leisurely lunch in a cosy pub, and wandered around the gardens of a local manor house, before picking up the car again.

'A lead had come adrift,' I told Murray casually. Driving back to town, I suggested, 'Let's see if Felix has knocked down that wall yet, shall we?' In truth, I intended to give him some encouragement on the Vestor front, but I offered him a very different explanation.

'Mrs. Young, who rents the flat above the shop, was away overnight, and Felix wanted to finish the wall before she got back.'

When we arrived, Felix was covered in dust, and still working. 'How's your foot?' Murray asked him.

'Badly bruised,' he replied, casting an injured look in my direction. 'Dropping a brick on it didn't help.'

I started to giggle, but Murray's interest was centred on a small niche in what was left of the wall. 'Hey, what's this?' He reached into the niche and as he pulled out a dust-covered tin box, the lid fell off, spilling the contents on the floor. 'Letters,' Murray exclaimed. Picking them up, he dusted them off, and gave a gasp. 'You'll never believe who they're from.' He showed me the name and address of the sender written on the back of the envelopes, which I read in wonder, just as if I'd never seen it before.

'Jeremiah Vestor. Wow!' I said, turning the envelopes over one by one. 'Look, Murray, they're all addressed to a Treasure May Crofton. Jeremiah's sweetheart! She must have lived in this very house before it became a shop.'

Murray whistled. 'That sure is some coincidence.'

'Life's full of 'em,' muttered Felix, heavy on the irony.

'Ignore him. He's just an old cynic,' I teased. 'In 1900 this was a very small town and Treasure had to live somewhere.'

I took Murray into the shop's small kitchen, while Felix got on with the wall, and as he sat reading the letters he became extremely excited. 'Jeremiah did return, Trish. His last letter states he was leaving for home on 16th May, 1902.'

'That's great. They probably married soon after. I'll check the records now I have a date to go on,' I waffled, like the expert he thought I was. 'I'll get it done by next Saturday. You will come back then, won't you?'

'Wild horses wouldn't keep me away,' he declared. For a moment he stood gazing out the window at the town. 'You know, Trish, perhaps I will take a look inside the abbey, after all.'

'You can't,' I blurted out. Not now things were going so well.

Swinging round, he looked deep into my eyes. 'Why ever not?'

'I meant, not this very minute. There's a service at this time.' Mum would have been proud of me. Women like us need to be quick thinkers.

'Another day then.'

I smiled shakily, thinking of the prominent plaque inside the abbey. The one dedicated to the memory of Treasure May Vestor, beloved wife of Jeremiah. Died, aged seventy-seven years.

Still, the information I'd carefully planted in the shop had intrigued him enough to make him want to return. And that's what mattered. Everything was going according to plan. Even the wall was finished by the time Murray was ready to leave for London. And as Felix and I stood at the door of the shop, saying goodbye to him, Mrs. Young arrived home from her overnight stay away. She looked at Murray and smiled, 'Hello. You found Trish all right then.'

'Mmm. As you see.'

'Did you find the plaque in the abbey?'

'Yes, I did.'

I felt my mouth drop open and he turned to me, his eyes alight with devilment. 'This is the lady I told you about. The one I met in the abbey churchyard, when I was looking at the gravestones. You'd rushed off to see your mother, if you remember.'

'I told him you were the best person to ask about the Vestors, Trish,' Mrs. Young said.

I choked and spluttered, 'That ---- that was kind of you.'

'Invaluable, I would say,' Murray agreed, chuckling, enjoying my obvious discomfort hugely.

Mrs. Young went up to her flat and Murray turned to us, saying quietly, 'I think someone owes me an explanation, don't you?'

'My cue to leave,' Felix muttered, grabbing his car keys. 'All I did was plant the letters like Trish asked.'

Murray shut the door after him and stood leaning against it, watching me intently. 'Who do the letters belong to, Trish?'

'My stepfather. His mother was a Vestor. The male line died out.' Then I exploded, 'Why didn't you tell me that you'd met Mrs. Young in the churchyard?'

He roared with laughter. 'What, and miss all the fun? I couldn't wait to see what you'd come up with next.'

He was far too intelligent not to guess the reason behind my subterfuge, and I saw no point in pretending otherwise. 'It's all very well for you. You're a man. If you fancy someone you can just----' His eyes were brimming with amusement, and I burst out, 'You have no idea what it's like for women like us.'

'Women like what?'

'Tall women with freckles, of course.'

'But, Trish,' he murmured softly, pulling me into his arms. 'I adore tall women with freckles. Why else would I have let you lead me on that crazy wild-goose chase?'

Oh honestly ---- isn't that just like a man!

Crime and the Councillor

Julian heard about the £10,000 through his voluntary work. He was involved in a new scheme, weaning disadvantaged teenagers away from vandalism and petty crime; teaching them a positive approach to life, a philosophy in which he whole-heartedly believed. He was also a local councillor, and being of use to the community was something he enjoyed.

Most of the kids he saw were rebellious rather than bad. They saw how other people lived, and were envious. And Julian, who had been out of a paid job for nearly a year, was shocked to find how much he identified with them. Redundancy had hit him harder than he'd realised.

As he told Sheila, his wife, 'If I was 30 years younger, I would be one of those kids.'

'No,' she insisted firmly. 'Not you.'

'How do you know? If I'd been brought up on a grotty, run-down estate, with no chance of a job.....'

She shook her head. 'You're far too intelligent.'

'Some of those lads are bright too, Sheila. They just don't know any other way of life.' He put his arms round her. 'They don't live in a lovely home in a pleasant, tree-lined avenue, as I do.' He nuzzled her hair. 'Nor do any of them have such a wonderful wife.'

'I've achieved something then,' Sheila teased, 'if I've kept you away from a life of crime!'

And it was true. Turning to crime wasn't an option for Julian. Or so he thought, until he overheard two of the boys discussing how to get their hands on this £10,000.

They were sitting side by side at a table, heads together, a tabloid newspaper open in front of them. Julian stood a few feet behind the boys, pinning an information sheet on the notice board. Only they were too engrossed in conversation to notice he was there.

'Look,' muttered the skinhead. 'It's easy, I tell you. There's this money left in Fielding's office safe over the weekend, see. Oh, come on, Brains, it's ten thousand quid. Just think what we could do with that! And all we have to do is find a way of pinching it.'

'Forget it.' Brains was adamant. 'What's the point? I don't know nothing about safes.'

The boys soon sauntered off to the snooker room, leaving Julian in a state of shock. Brains might not know anything about safes, but *he* did. He'd spent the last 25 years installing them. Happy years, in a job he'd loved.

With his inside knowledge, he knew exactly how to rob a safe – a fact he'd never given a thought to before. But he was thinking about it now all right. He sat down at the table where the boys had sat, his eyes on the newspaper, but his mind was on the £10,000. And how much he wanted it.

He even found himself considering how the robbery could be done. Of course, the whole enterprise would need careful preparation. But was he up to it? The first thing, he decided, was to make detailed drawings of the premises, the position of the safe, and the alarm systems. Success would depend on his ingenuity. No weapons, of course. He didn't agree with violence. The more he thought about it, the more convinced he became that he could do it.

Naturally he thought about his family too. Sheila was a bank manager, their grown-up son had just joined the police force, and he, himself, was a councillor, a highly respected figure in the community, who got things done. Well, if he hadn't been made redundant he'd never have given crime a moment's thought.

If he went for it, there'd be no more aimless killing of time, no more applying for jobs to companies who often didn't even have the courtesy to reply; no more putting on a cheerful front, pretending he didn't mind being out of work. This would be a test. If he pulled it off, he could carve a whole new career out of crime.

When Julian got home, Sheila took one look at his sparkling eyes, kissed him and queried with warm affection, 'What have you been up to, you old devil?' She hadn't seen that look of purpose for far too long.

Laughing, he hugged her. 'Oh, nothing really, love. It's just this project with the boys putting new life into me. I feel as if I'm doing something useful again.' Having never kept anything from her before, he felt decidedly guilty.

But she just sighed thankfully. 'Didn't I tell you work wasn't everything in life?'

'Frequently, my darling,' he grinned. 'Without you, my love, I reckon I would have gone under. You're always there when I need you, helping, advising. Loving me,' he murmured. 'I'm a very lucky man.' He'd tell her the truth if it came off. If it didn't..... He shrugged. He'd worry about that if it happened.

Once the first euphoria had passed, of course, he'd discovered the project wasn't as easy as he'd thought. But it wasn't in his nature to give up. In the end, the outcome surprised even him. Naturally, he'd given considerable thought to where success, or failure, would lead. But at no time did it occur to Julian that his photograph would be plastered across the front of a daily newspaper. That same tabloid the boys had left on the table.

COUNCILLOR TURNS TO CRIME screamed the headline. And the photograph was positively sinister. Sheila, who now knew what he'd done, leaned over his shoulder and began reading the report.......

'A large sum of money left in Fielding's office safe over the weekend had disappeared when staff arrived on Monday. There was no sign of a break-in.' She paused. *'From this beginning, contestants in the paper's recent short story competition were asked for entertaining and believable stories on how this crime was carried out.'* Sheila went on proudly, *'And we are pleased to announce that Julian Black's highly ingenious and amusing entry wins the £10,000 prize.'*

When Lightning Strikes

Sometimes sisters are a real pain. Take mine; with three children all under five, Kate ought to be too exhausted to worry about my love life. And definitely too exhausted to organise dinner parties.

'Just a few friends,' she says. 'And this gorgeous man.' She ignores my loud groan. 'Honestly, Lowri, you'll like Tim. Soft grey-blue eyes, nice teeth, well-dressed, good manners, owns a lovely house and car, and adores kids.' She barely pauses to catch her breath. 'Lost his wife five years ago, no children.'

'Did you employ a private detective?' I ask. 'Or did he fill in a questionnaire?'

She giggles, then returns to the attack. 'Tim's perfect, Lowri.'

They always are. 'No thanks,' I say. 'I'm busy that night.'

She glares at me. 'But I haven't told you when it is yet.'

'It doesn't matter. I won't be there, Kate.'

She studies her nails. 'There'll be poached salmon and my special double chocolate pudding.'

Two of my favourite dishes, and Kate's a marvellous cook. An involuntary, 'When?' escapes my lips.

'Friday.'

Her smile is maddeningly smug, but Friday is exactly as I expect. The food is perfect and the man is pleasant in both looks and conversation, but when it comes to love, he's as uninterested in me as I am in him.

I know exactly the kind of man I'm looking for. I manage a local leisure centre, I love sports and I'm a keen hill walker. Tim adores classical music, ballet, the theatre and he runs an art gallery.

On parting, Tim and I utter the polite hope that we'll meet again. I get into the car and, while Tim thanks my brother-in-law, Kate hisses, 'Aren't you going to ask for his phone number?'

I shake my head and turn on the ignition key. Nothing happens. I try again. Not a spark. Rather like Tim and me. Hope springs into Kate's eyes, and before I can stop her, she's asked Tim to take me home.

'No, really,' I protest, flustered. 'It's too far out of your way.' He lives seven miles to the east, and my flat's ten miles westwards. But Kate isn't listening. She bundles me into Tim's car.

As we move off, Tim begins the polite small talk. 'Kate is so thoughtful....'

'Kate,' I say furiously, 'is an interfering busybody who will stoop to any depths to throw us together --- including sabotaging my car.'

His lips twitch. 'And there was I hoping for a goodnight kiss. At the very least,' he adds provocatively.

I look across at him and his eyes are dancing with mischief. 'I guess that was rather blunt of me,' I admit. 'But I prefer to speak the truth. Mind you, according to Kate, that's why I'm still single.'

He turns into the main road. 'Well, perhaps you haven't met anyone you really cared for, yet.'

'No-one I can't live without.' Catching a fleeting glimpse of pain on his face I remember too late that he's a widower. 'I'm sorry, Tim. That was really thoughtless of me.'

'No need to apologise.' We stop at traffic lights and he smiles. 'The right person is worth waiting for, Lowri, believe me. The instant I saw Jenny I just knew I would marry her. It was like lightning striking......'

'Yes,' I break in eagerly, 'love should be like that, shouldn't it?' The lights change and we move on. 'What made Kate think we'd hit it off? We don't have a single thing in common.'

'Heaven knows. Tell me, Lowri, do you really enjoy hill walking in all weathers?' he shudders.

'I love it.' Ruefully I add, 'Sorry, but I know nothing about painting or art. I can't tell Monet from Manet, or Gauguin from Van Gogh. Except that Gauguin kept both his ears.'

Laughing, he promises, 'I'll willingly teach you any time.'

We draw up outside my flat and I thank him. 'It's been nice meeting you.'

'How polite,' he teases, grinning at me.

I smile. 'I do have a few social graces, you know.' And we say goodbye.

Kate vehemently denies sabotaging my car, but when she hears I'm not meeting Tim again, she swears she'll never cook me another double chocolate pudding in her life. 'If you can turn down someone as perfect as Tim, I wash my hands of you.'

Life goes on. I play badminton, squash, hockey, go hill walking..... Then, about a month later, I pop into my favourite cafe for a coffee and bump into Tim.

He grins at me. 'Been to any dinner parties lately?'

Kate's vow was predictably short-lived. 'The last one was an Italian bum-pincher,' I tell him, and he shakes with laughter.

Then he says, 'You think you've had it rough. My mother once tried to fix me up with a lady wrestler!' I splutter into my coffee cup. 'Mother's getting desperate. She says she wants grandchildren before she pops off.'

'How old is she?' I ask, picturing a white-haired old lady crocheting in a rocking chair.

'Fifty-seven, and as fit as a fiddle. She ran in the London Marathon last year.' I burst out laughing and he joins in. 'The trouble is, I haven't seen the last of Muscle woman yet. I'm best man at a friend's wedding on Saturday and she's chief bridesmaid.' He goes on gloomily, 'There's a ceilidh afterwards and I just *know* I'll end up partnering her.....' He stops, and looks at me with a glint of hope in his eyes. 'Unless....' he breathes, 'Lowri, would you be my partner? That's if you're not camping on some awful snow-swept mountain this weekend.'

'But *I'm* not invited.'

'My invitation states "and friend."' His eyes plead with me. Kate's right, they are a lovely grey-blue. 'Look, we might not have fallen in love, but we do get on, don't we?' I stare at him. 'Do this for me, and I'll be your partner when you need one. If it works, well, we can make it a permanent arrangement.'

The ceilidh is fun. And during the next few months Tim and I escort each other to a variety of functions, becoming really good friends in the process. We tell no-one the truth about our arrangement, and it works wonders.

Tim's mother and Kate cut out the matchmaking. Yet, thankfully, double chocolate pudding remains a staple part of my diet, because Kate regularly invites us both to dinner, to check on how our "romance" is progressing. Of course, we do have to lie a little. Like the time Kate crows, 'Didn't I say Tim was perfect for you?'

Lowering my eyes, I nod, and she nudges me slyly, 'What's he like in bed then?' I blink, taken completely by surprise. 'Oh, come on, Lowri, you can tell me. I am your sister, after all.'

Giggling, I assure her, 'Like you say --- he's perfect, in *every* way.'

When I tell Tim later, he rolls his eyes at me. 'And my mother wants to know when we're getting married.' We howl with laughter. Fooling the matchmakers is enormously satisfying. And it need only stop when one of us falls in love. What could be more civilised? And, of course, it leaves us both free to go out with whoever we like. Unfortunately, I'd reckoned without Kate.

I'm having a quiet drink with a handsome hunk I'd met at the leisure centre, when who should walk in but Kate and my brother-in-law. They're with friends, but Kate storms straight over, her bosom heaving with indignation. I introduce her to Dwight, and she instantly demands in a loud righteous voice, 'And how's Tim?'

'He's fine, thanks,' I assure her calmly.

Furious at my lack of concern, she rejoins her party, but casts frequent scandalised glares of disapproval in my direction. I arrive home at midnight and the phone is ringing. 'Are you alone?' Kate growls, emphasising the 'alone' so dramatically, I have to suppress a giggle.

'I am. Look, Kate, Tim and I are not tied to each other's apron strings.'

'When you love a man, Lowri,' she declares primly, 'you simply do not do that sort of thing.'

I relate the whole episode to Tim the next day, on our way to have dinner with his mother. Tim doesn't laugh as I expect, but the traffic is bad and he's concentrating on his driving. 'Is this it then, Lowri?' he finally asks. 'Are you in love?'

There's an edge to his voice, but I know what's worrying him. He's scared I won't need him any more and he'll be at the mercy of the matchmakers again. 'Don't worry, Tim, I haven't been struck by lightning, if that's what you mean.'

Tim draws up outside his mother's house. 'Lowri....' he begins, twisting the car keys so nervously in his hands that I stare at him in amazement. I've never seen him like this before. 'People don't always fall in love at first sight, do they? I mean, sometimes, love grows. Two people start by liking each other and....'

'Maybe.' I pat his knee and he looks at me with an expression I can't fathom in the darkness. 'Honestly, Tim, I can't see that happening with Dwight and me. When I meet the right man, I'll know it, believe me.'

He doesn't answer and I ask in concern, 'Tim, is anything wrong? I haven't put my foot in it anywhere along the line, have I?'

There's a pause. 'Of course not. Everything's fine.'

Every Monday, Kate and I lunch together, invariably in the same restaurant. Which means I have to walk past Tim's art gallery. This Monday, there's a lulu of a thunderstorm going on, but I decide to pop in to the gallery just to make sure Tim really is all right, that I haven't inadvertently upset him. He's part of my life now and I really don't want that to change.

I'm about to cross the road, when Tim comes out with his arm around a gorgeous blonde. They stand in the doorway, out of the rain, holding hands and talking a while. They kiss on parting and he goes back into the gallery.

Lightning flashes madly as I stand transfixed, grappling with this totally unexpected, yet utterly overwhelming desire to scratch her eyes out. I forget everything except Tim. I cross over the road and burst into the gallery.

'This *is* a pleasant surprise,' Tim smiles, And teases, 'Have you come to learn about art?'

Shaking my head, I gulp, 'That woman. Just now. Outside....'

'Yes?' And his eyes are fixed intently on my face.

My voice falters, 'Do....do you love her?'

He takes my hands and I feel a sudden shiver of delight. 'Would it matter to you if I did?' There's an expression in his eyes I can't mistake, and it gives me the courage to say, 'Of course it matters, you idiot. Tim ---- I don't think I can live without you.'

'My wonderful blunt Lowri, don't ever change,' he mutters thickly, before crushing me in his arms.

Between kisses, he whispers, 'When you met Dwight, I thought I'd lost you.'

When we join Kate at the restaurant later, I learn the blonde was her idea. Kate laughs. 'I always knew Tim was perfect for you, and someone had to bring you together.'

Tim grins. 'Kate, you are a very wise woman.'

And just this once, I have to agree.

Jordie

With five babies to be christened that Sunday, the beautiful Norman village church was full. But far from quiet, with several restless toddlers and crying babies. As I wasn't a godmother, I stood well back from the font. The vicar had just taken my latest nephew in his arms, when I felt something wet hit the back of my neck.

Whirling round, my suspicions were instantly aroused by the pious faces of several small boys standing not far behind me. Determined to find the culprit, I slowly inched my way through the throng to the very back, where I watched and waited. Sure enough, before long, an angelic-looking child of about six produced a water pistol. As he took aim at a rather large, flamboyant hat, I sidled up to him and hissed out of the side of my mouth, 'Okay, Buster, the game's up.'

I tried not to laugh as he hurriedly hid the pistol behind his back. 'Where are your parents?' I whispered.

'They're dead,' he said, his voice wobbling alarmingly.

Horrified that I'd upset him, I crouched down to his level and tried to make amends. 'I'm sorry. What's your name?'

'Jordan.'

'Mine's Alexandra. Sandy for short.' I smiled at him. 'Who did you come with, Jordan?' He pointed to the font, where the godparents stood. 'Which one?' I asked.

He pointed again. 'Him. The vicar,' Jordan said, as if I was a halfwit. 'He's my uncle.'

I looked at the vicar properly for the first time and saw a grown-up version of Jordan, with black curls, good looks and a roguish grin. 'He won't like you playing with a water pistol in church,' I pointed out. Jordan hung his head. 'Save it for later,' I advised gently.

'Okay. The water's all gone now anyway.'

I went back to my place, and watched the rest of the service. Afterwards, as people began to leave, the boy next to Jordan screamed, 'Jordan kicked me.'

'You broke my water pistol,' Jordan burst out.

The vicar hurried over and sorted it out in a sensible way, while I picked up the pieces of the toy. 'Can I have another water pistol, please?' Jordan begged.

'Only if you promise not to bring it to church,' the vicar warned. Turning to me, he laughed, 'Children!'

I hadn't met this vicar before, but I liked Neil Hawkins on sight. 'Is Jordan here on holiday?' I asked.

Neil's eyes clouded over. 'No. He lives with me now. Permanently.'

He glanced at his nephew, who muttered, 'I told her about Mum and Dad.' Neil squeezed his shoulder comfortingly. 'Uncle, I won't have to come to church again tonight, will I?'

Neil sighed. 'Afraid so, old son.' He told me, 'My fiancée was to have sat with Jordie today, but she – er – couldn't.' So Neil was spoken for. I might have known. It was just my luck.

'They had a row,' Jordan interpreted, matter-of-factly. 'Lauren doesn't like me.'

Neil interrupted, 'Of course she likes you.'

'She said I'm....' he screwed up his face trying to remember the word. 'I'm a noxious brat.'

'Obnoxious,' grinned Neil, putting an arm around Jordan's shoulders. 'And so you are,' he teased.

There was no mistaking the love each held for the other. Also, it was clear I'd stumbled into their lives at a critical point. 'I could sit with Jordan this evening,' I offered.

Neil was doubtful. 'Well....'

'I have ten nieces and nephews,' I told him, smiling. 'I'm used to looking after children.'

'Oh, please,' begged Jordan. 'I like Sandy.'

Neil roared with laughter. 'That settles it, then. If you're sure?'

Now why had I been so eager to help I asked myself severely, on the way home. As if I didn't know perfectly well! Although I'd have sat with Jordan willingly, even if Neil had been white-haired and pot-bellied. For, unless I was much mistaken, Jordan needed all the help he could get right now.

But I'd almost fallen over myself with eagerness, because of Neil's black curls and roguish grin. And I'd conveniently ignored the one word he'd spoken that stood between us. Fiancée. Such a small word too. Seven letters, denoting that he'd entered into a promise to marry. No man made that promise lightly. Least of all a vicar. I was in danger of making a bigger fool of myself than usual. But I headed straight for the precipice anyway.

When I returned to the vicarage that evening, Neil told me that Jordan's parents had been killed in a car crash four weeks earlier. 'It's Jordie who's suffering most, of course,' he sighed. 'I'm the only family he has now.'

'I can see you get on really well.'

'He's a great kid.' He smiled at me and my heart did a triple somersault. 'Thanks for coming to the rescue. It's the feminine touch Jordie misses the most.'

'Surely your fiancée will solve that.' Oh, I can be virtuous when I have to be. Anyway, I wanted to find out why Jordie didn't like Lauren.

He hesitated. 'Yes, I – er --- I like to think so.'

So there was a problem. 'Have you been engaged long?' Well, I had to know what I was up against, didn't I?

'Two months,' he said, in answer to my question. 'Not long after we met, actually. Love at first sight,' he smiled. Tell me about it, I thought, as I fought an overpowering urge to smooth back the black curl escaping round his ear. Neil was, quite rightly, keeping his difficulties to himself. In fairness, I had to admit the unexpected addition of a small boy would put a strain on most relationships. But, by the time I'd put Jordie to bed that night, it wasn't only Neil who'd captured my heart.

After I'd read Jordie a story, he threw his arms round my neck. 'S...Sandy,' he began haltingly, and I felt his whole body quiver, 'you're wearing the same perfume as my mum.' Then he began to sob. Huge, heart-rending sounds, that tore me apart. I held him tightly in my arms, rocking him gently, and smoothing his hair, until he finally stopped crying.

'Oh, Jordie,' I choked, hugging him. 'Would you rather I didn't wear that perfume?'

'No,' he said at once, looking at me from under dark, wet lashes. 'Uncle Neil says I must always remember everything I can about my mum and dad.'

'Uncle Neil is right,' I said.

I'd wondered what Lauren was like, and told myself that if she turned out to be nice after all, I must do the decent thing and back out. But when Neil returned from church, bringing Lauren with him, I saw at once that backing out wasn't a matter of choice --- it was my only option. Lauren was the most gorgeous creature I'd ever seen. As for competing against her, I had more chance of flying to Mars.

Within half an hour I had Lauren all figured out. I knew exactly why Jordie didn't like her. And why she wasn't right for Neil. She oozed charm, yet her smile never reached her eyes. Those huge blue orbs were as hard as nails. I guess even a clergyman can be blinded by glamour. Frankly, it surprised me that she'd settled for a mere vicar. Until she let drop that her father was a bishop. I understood then. Neil was to go far.

The things Jordie needed, like love and affection, weren't part of her plan. If I'd had any sense, I would have left for good then, but I couldn't just abandon the child to his fate. One raw deal in life was enough for any six year old. So I offered to take Jordie to my parents' house the following Sunday, to our weekly family gathering. 'He can play with my nieces and nephews,' I said. If it meant heartache for me, then so be it. That child badly needed a break. Something to help him over the trauma he'd suffered.

Lauren was delighted. 'That would be wonderful, wouldn't it, Neil?'

Neil frowned. 'I wouldn't like to impose on your family.'

'You won't be,' I said, smiling. And added pointedly, 'My parents love to see children enjoying themselves.' Lauren didn't even blink.

Jordie loved our family gathering so much, I took him every Sunday after that. In those weeks my love for Neil grew and deepened. He still seemed unaware of Lauren's true character and plans for their wedding went ahead. What could I do? I mean, how do you tell a man his fiancée will ruin the life of a child, and probably his own too? I forced myself to face the truth. In two months, Lauren would become Mrs Neil Hawkins, and it would be goodbye Sandy. There was nothing I could do about it.

The following Sunday, hiding my despair from Jordie, I showed him the kittens newly born to our family cat. With shining eyes he said, 'Do you think Uncle Neil will let me have a kitten?'

'Ask him,' I said, smiling. It seemed to me a cat would give Jordie something to love and care for. Something to take his mind off the tragedy. But I'd reckoned without Lauren.

'No!' she stormed at Jordie, greatly agitated. 'There'll be no cats in this house.'

Stunned, Neil said, 'Surely we can talk about it.....'

Seeing the disapproval on his face, she sat on his lap, playfully messing up his hair. 'I'm sorry, darling,' she purred, as I clenched my fists tightly to stop myself scratching her eyes out, 'but cats catch mice and bring them into the house. Alive,' she said with a shudder. 'You know I'm terrified of mice.'

To my astonishment, Neil shoved her off his lap and hurried over to Jordie, who stood with silent tears running down his cheeks. When Neil tried to hug him, Jordie pushed him away, and in a voice filled with loathing, yelled, 'I hate Lauren. I *hate* her.'

Eventually, at Neil's insistence, Jordie apologised. He remained subdued, however, but when Lauren stood up to leave, he offered to fetch her coat. After he'd left the room, Neil said to Lauren, 'I think you owe Jordie an apology too. There was no need to scream at him.'

'Apologise to a child?' she protested. I could see she was desperately trying to keep calm, but her face was still white with rage, even when Jordie returned with her coat.

He'd been gone rather a long time, but I didn't think anything of it until Lauren put the coat on. There was a small bulge in one pocket, which she immediately investigated. Jordie could hardly contain his glee when she pulled out a mouse by its tail. Eyes wide with horror, she screamed, dropping the mouse, and continued to scream as it landed upright and shot across the floor to the skirting board. Where it came to an abrupt halt.

'It's only a toy,' I spluttered. Well, someone had to stop her screaming and Neil was too busy trying not to laugh.

Eventually he managed to speak. 'Try to see the funny side, Lauren. It's only a silly joke.'

'Oh, is it?' she shrieked. 'And that makes it all right, I suppose. I think that child means more to you than I do.'

He looked at her for a moment without speaking, and then said with quiet regret, 'Yes, I'm afraid he does.'

With nostrils flaring, she pulled off her engagement ring and threw it at Neil's feet. 'Daddy was right. You'll never amount to anything. You're too soft.' And she flounced out, slamming the door behind her.

I longed to cheer, but Jordie was far more practical. He asked hopefully, 'Can I have a kitten now?'

Neil choked back a laugh. 'After what you've just done?' But the twinkle in his eyes said Jordie would get his cat.

'Would you like me to put Jordie to bed?' I asked.

Neil shook his head, and the look in his eyes made my heart lurch. He turned to his nephew. 'Jordie, I want to speak to Sandy alone for a few minutes.'

Jordie burst out excitedly, 'Are you going to ask Sandy to marry you now?'

We both gasped, and Neil said, 'Life isn't always that simple, I'm afraid.'

Cheekily he grinned. 'But she likes you, Uncle Neil. Don't you Sandy?'

'I...er...,' I looked up to find Neil watching me intently, and I went crimson.

Jordie begged, 'Come and live with us, Sandy. Ple—a—se.'

Neil walked Jordie to the door and opened it. 'Out!' he ordered cheerfully. 'Go upstairs and tidy your room.'

Shutting the door again, he turned back to me. 'I'm sorry about that. I mean....you probably have a boyfriend.' When I shook my head, his eyes brightened. 'Oh good. I..er...began to realise a few weeks ago that I'd made a terrible mistake with Lauren.' He added ruefully, 'I was dazzled by her, I suppose. Unlike Jordie-- he saw through her straight away.'

'Children do.'

He was looking at me in a way that set my heart pounding so loudly I was convinced he would hear it. 'Just lately, Sandy,' he said, 'whenever the doorbell rang, it was you I hoped to see, not Lauren.'

I was too choked with emotion to speak, but I smiled at him and my eyes must have said it all anyway, for he took two swift strides towards me. At that moment, the door opened again and Jordie stood there grinning. 'Are you going to kiss her, Uncle Neil?'

'I do hope so,' I said fervently. And walked joyfully into his open arms.

Red Herrings

The sign on our office door stood out in bold, clear lettering: *Baker Street Detective Agency.* Underneath were the office hours, followed by an invitation to enter. At five minutes past nine the door opened and I looked up hopefully. When an attractive, long-legged blonde sauntered in, I sighed in disappointment. 'Oh, it's you. I thought it was a client.'

It had been six months since Tara and I, after years spent working for other people, set up on our own in Baker Street – surely the perfect location for a detective agency. OK, so it wasn't the Baker Street of Sherlock Holmes fame. It wasn't even in London. But let's not get too picky, eh?

I organised our schedule, when we had one. Today, we didn't. Tara perched herself on the corner of my desk and asked the question I'd been dreading. 'Kirstie, exactly how much work do we have on?'

'You mean, right now?'

Tara nodded, and I chewed the end of my pen, praying the phone would ring, or a client would appear. But nothing happened. 'None,' I muttered.

What we needed was some good publicity. One really successful case, with our names in the newspapers, and we'd be made. But, right now, that seemed as likely as us orbiting the earth on a tandem. 'It's not fair,' I burst out, thumping my fist on the desk so hard that all the pens leapt into the air.

'Oh well, that's life, I guess,' Tara said with a shrug. Not much fazed Tara. It was an asset in our professional lives, but her calm acceptance of our failure made me so livid, I picked up one of Conan Doyle's masterpieces and threw it at the door.

At that precise moment the door opened --- and the man who entered caught the missile deftly with his left hand. In our business we learn to assess people on sight and, even as I jumped out of my chair, I mentally ticked honest, sensible, confident and caring.

Physically he was fairly ordinary, but I liked the wide, sensitive mouth and laughing brown eyes. He had nice hands too, with clean, square-cut nails. He was that rare species of man --- my type. 'I'm so sorry,' I said, flushing with embarrassment.

'Slipped out of your hand?' he inquired with a grin, returning the book to me.

I laughed. 'Something like that. Um --- can I help you?'

Smiling, he sat down opposite me. 'I certainly hope so.'

I took a deep breath. 'I should tell you we're an all female agency.' Well, why waste time?

His lips quivered in amusement. 'That's why I've come to you.'

'Really?' I gasped.

Tara the unfazed took over. 'What can we do for you, Mr---?'

'Smith. Gordon Smith. And I want you to find the man who's threatening to, er --- bump me off.'

I blinked, and asked him how the threats had been communicated. 'By my landline phone,' he said. 'The man's voice was obviously disguised, and he withheld his number. My number, incidentally, is ex-directory. And to be perfectly honest,' he confessed ruefully, 'I find it all rather unnerving.'

'Not nice,' I agreed. 'Did he give a reason?'

'Mmmm. It's rather bizarre really. I earn my living writing detective fiction, you see.'

Tara's eyes widened. 'Should we know you?'

He told us his pseudonym. We knew him all right. A rising star, the critics said. 'Anyway,' he went on, 'this screwball accused me of stealing the plot of my latest book from him. To be exact, from a manuscript he'd sent to me. But when I refused to compensate him, he threatened to kill me.'

'Why would he send you his manuscript?' I inquired, puzzled.

He shrugged. 'There's always someone who thinks I can help them get a publishing deal. But my secretary would have returned it to him immediately, with advice on how to approach a publisher. I never even saw his manuscript, so any similarity between his book and mine is pure coincidence.' I nodded and he said, 'The police advised me to take the threat seriously, which is why I've come to you. Because for the next three weeks I'll be cruising out to the Caribbean and back, lecturing on detective fiction. As this crank is a writer he could be----'

'On the ship,' I cut in. 'And at your lectures.'

'Precisely.' He ran a hand through his hair. 'Someone that unbalanced needs to be caught quickly. And I reckon female investigators would be less obtrusive on a cruise ship.' I could feel my jaw dropping, and Tara's eyes were out on stalks. 'Do you have anyone available at such short notice?' he asked uncertainly. 'All expenses paid, of course, plus your fee. The cruise line has been both co-operative and generous. On account of a murdered guest lecturer being bad publicity,' he ended with a grin.

As he sat waiting for an answer, I held our appointment book upright, ran a finger down the blank pages, slammed it shut and smiled. 'Our other agents are tied up at present, but Tara and I can manage it.'

After all, what did we have to lose? If this crackpot was on the ship and we nailed him, the Baker Street Detective Agency would take off like a rocket. If he wasn't, at least we'd get a free Caribbean cruise. Before we went bankrupt.

So I took note of all the usual personal details, explaining, 'It's important to have an overall picture.'

When I asked if he was married, he said, 'Yes, but I'm separated. The divorce is going ahead, now that my wife's finally accepted a financial settlement that doesn't leave me destitute.'

Tara commented on the unusual design of the ring he was wearing and he said, 'My wife had it made for me when we married. Designing jewellery is one of her hobbies. I've always liked it, which is why I still wear it occasionally.'

Not many people would come out of a bad marriage so well-adjusted, I reflected. I handed him a Baker Street Detective

Agency card and introduced myself properly. 'I'm Kirstie Watson.'

'*Watson?*' he spluttered, amused. 'Oh, come on, you can't expect me to swallow that.' Silently I produced a copy of my birth certificate, kept in my desk for unbelievers. 'Kirstie Elizabeth Watson,' he read out loud, and instantly turned to Tara, his eyes alight with laughter. 'Then, of course, you must be Holmes.'

She smiled. 'Tara Blenkinsop, actually.'

A few days later, along with hundreds of other passengers, we leant over the rail of the cruise liner, throwing streamers onto the quayside, while the band played "*Sailing.*" As we sailed majestically down Southampton Water, Tara said dreamily, 'I'm really going to enjoy this. Just think, three whole weeks of sun and sea. What more could a girl want?'

'Romance?' I suggested.

Tara giggled. 'If I can find a suitable hunk. I mean, I won't get a look-in with Gordon, will I?' she teased, fluttering her eyelashes at me meaningfully. 'Not with you around.'

I laughed. 'He's not interested.' And he wasn't. Not yet. His wife had given him too rough a time. But I could wait. 'First,' I reminded her, 'we have to nail this nutter.'

Our plan was to sit in on Gordon's lectures, pretending to be budding writers. If our man was there, it would be easy to suss him out. He'd be a loner; these types usually were. But none of the men in the group showed any hostility towards Gordon. Not even in their body language, which is how people usually give themselves away.

We attended every lecture as we crossed the Atlantic, and kept tabs on Gordon whenever he was outside his cabin, and still no-one gave us the slightest cause for suspicion. So why did I feel so uneasy?

Once we reached the Caribbean, Gordon suggested to me that Tara and I should relax our vigil and enjoy ourselves. 'If that madman was on the ship, he would have tried his luck by now.'

When I told Tara, she was ecstatic, having found her shipboard romance in the shape of a very handsome, fun-loving London stockbroker called Dean. The four of us spent a lot of time together.

'Don't get too excited,' I warned her. 'I refused.'

'You did *what?*' she gasped, astounded.

'Tara, if anything happened to Gordon while we were.......'

She snorted. 'Don't give me that. You just want an excuse to be near him.'

I shook my head. 'It's not that.' I took a deep breath. 'I can't get this feeling out of my mind that we've missed something.'

Her eyes widened, but she didn't laugh. In our business intuition was something we'd learned to trust. 'OK,' she capitulated, 'we'll keep things as they are then. With just the four of us.'

If Dean minded, he didn't show it. Spending so much time with us, we'd had to explain to him about Gordon, or we couldn't have talked about it in front of him. He was clearly shocked and offered to help, making a great show of flexing his muscles. He certainly looked fit; useful if an attempt was made on Gordon's life. He was fun too, and just grinned when we teased him about his collection of pendants. He had enough to open a shop and never wore the same one twice.

Returning across the Atlantic, Gordon resumed his lectures, which I continued to attend. Tara said it was simply an excuse to sit gazing at him. But the truth was I enjoyed the talks. Particularly the one on red herrings. Which, Gordon informed us, played an essential role in detective stories, being a ploy the culprit used to throw the fictional detective off the scent. It was all fascinating stuff but, as I told Gordon afterwards, 'I don't come across many red herrings in my line of work.'

We were making our way down the carpeted stairs to our cabins at the time, and he grinned at me. 'Ah, but fiction should be more exciting than real life, surely?'

I suddenly missed my footing and lurched towards him. He caught me in his arms, and I knew which of those choices I found more exciting. And it wasn't fiction. I was still trembling when I reached the cabin.

Dean and Tara joined the rush for places on the sundeck that afternoon. Meanwhile, Gordon and I settled for the cooler promenade deck, sitting with our feet on the rail, watching the flying fish, lulled by the gentle movement of the ship. Surely Gordon was safe while someone was with him? Yet the hairs on the back of my neck continued to warn me he was in great danger.

Again and again I sifted the evidence in my mind, but it wasn't until I was dressing for the Captain's cocktail party that the answer hit me. And it took my breath away. Tara glanced at me. 'Hey, are you all right, Kirstie? You're as white as a sheet.'

'Tara, if anything happened to Gordon, where do you think we would start looking for the culprit?'

'Among the writing fraternity, of course.'

'And why is that?'

'Because, Dumbo,' she said patiently, 'the man who made those threats is a writer.'

'That's what he told Gordon, yes,' I muttered grimly. 'And not one of us questioned it.'

'But,' she protested, zipping up her black cocktail dress, 'he accused Gordon of pinching his plot.'

'Yes, I know. But what if that was a red herring? A means of covering up the real motive? I don't think our quarry is some nutty writer,' I persisted. 'I think he's quite sane and deadly serious. And, what's more, he's on this ship.'

She stared at me, not laughing now. 'If you're right, Kirstie, that would make us two very dumb detectives.'

'Yes,' I gulped. I was suddenly very frightened.

'Where's Gordon right now?' Tara asked.

'In his cabin.' He wasn't bothering with the Captain's cocktail party. 'He's safe enough there.'

A knock on our door made us both jump. Tara answered it and said in relief, 'Oh, it's you.'

Dean came in, still wearing shirt and shorts. 'Thought I'd better warn you, we must be heading for bad weather. The sick bags are everywhere.' We groaned and he grinned – he'd never been seasick in his life – and he asked Tara, 'What time is this blessed cocktail party? I've lost my invitation.'

'In half an hour,' she told him. 'And at this rate you're going to be late.'

'Not me. I'll be changed in a jiffy. I don't need two hours like you girls.'

'Well, hurry up then. Gordon's not going so we need you to escort us.'

'You can rely on me, ma'am.' He swept an exaggerated low bow, and the light caught the pendant he was wearing, showing up an unusual design I'd seen before somewhere......

Once he'd gone, we returned to our sleuthing. 'We're dealing with someone very clever here,' I said. 'Tara, if you'd planted that red herring, what would you do next?'

She thought for a moment. 'Befriend Gordon in a way that wouldn't look suspicious.'

I searched for an example. 'Like...Dean?'

She glared at me. 'Kirstie, you're not suggesting.....'

'No, of course not. Go on.'

'Then I'd get all matey---'

'Like Dean?' I teased.

'Oh, shut up. Then, once Gordon trusted me, I'd push him overboard or something.' She looked out at the sunset. 'About now, when the light's going and everyone's changing for the Captain's cocktail party.'

'Everyone ---- except De-a-n.' I felt my mouth drop open--- I'd just remembered why the design on Dean's pendant was familiar. I'd seen it before, on the ring Gordon sometimes wore. The one his wife had designed.

When I told Tara, she shrugged. 'So what?'

'Gordon said designing jewellery was his wife's hobby. You can't buy her stuff in a shop.'

She stared at me, opening and closing her mouth like a goldfish. Finally, she burst out, 'Do you realise what you're saying?'

I nodded. 'I do. Gordon's wife must have given Dean that pendant.'

'But they don't know each other.' I didn't answer and she just looked at me, then her bottom lip wobbled and she pleaded shakily, 'Kirstie, why would she do that?'

I heaved a long, weary sigh. 'Do you want me to draw you a picture?' She still shook her head, so I had to give it to her straight. 'Tara, if Gordon dies before the divorce goes through, who would get all his money?'

'No,' she whispered, shaking her head vehemently. 'Dean wouldn't.....he wouldn't.' The unfazeable Tara was finally fazed. She was too shocked to see the purpose behind the red herring. That, in the event of Gordon's demise, the police would naturally start a hunt for an unhinged writer, not for a vindictive, money-grabbing wife and her lover.

Two minutes later we burst into Gordon's cabin, and found him having a quiet drink with Dean on his private veranda, an area of deck between the cabin and the rail. The relief I felt at finding him safe was unimaginable, but I caught the flicker of anger in Dean's eyes. If I'd had any doubts that look removed them.

Dean was still wearing the shorts and shirt we'd seen him in earlier. 'What are you two doing here?' He smiled lazily. 'You won't persuade Gordon to go to the cocktail party, I'm afraid. I've tried.'

Gordon leaned back in his chair, his eyes telling me everything was fine. That he knew. 'I rather think, Dean, that Kirstie expected to find you dumping my inert body overboard.'

Dean choked.

'And given another few minutes,' Gordon continued, 'I imagine you'd have tried.'

Dean staggered to his feet, knocking his chair over, his face ashen. He stretched his hands out to Tara. 'Surely, you don't think.....?' Tara didn't speak. She simply snatched the pendant roughly from Dean's neck, and put it beside the ring Gordon handed to her.

'After that,' Gordon whispered into my ear, 'it was elementary, wasn't it, my dear Watson?'

The Baker Street Detective Agency did indeed become a roaring success, but it was months before I saw Gordon again. He walked into the office one day and smiled at me in a manner that got my heart thumping like a set of bongo drums. 'Now that I'm a free man again,' he said, 'I wondered if you would be interested in another investigation. Of a more personal nature,' he ended softly.

'Oh, I *would*,' I sighed. Well, why be subtle? I'd waited a long time.

'Good.' He grinned at me and suggested, 'Dinner this evening? I know the perfect place.'

He did too. A fish restaurant. I didn't notice the name of it until the waiter handed me a menu. It was called *The Red Herring*.

The Wedding Jinx

Today, Easter Saturday, is my wedding day and I'm as jumpy as a blindfolded volunteer in a knife-throwing act. Believe me, I have good reason to fear calamity. Weddings in our family are jinxed.

Mind you, to the family, the jinx is a hoot. Waves of hysterical, infectious laughter reverberate into the street at the mention of the word 'wedding.' They call us the Mad Lovedays. An apt description for a bunch of fun-loving Geordies. Father is a popular primary school head teacher. Mother is involved with several charities, and there are six grown-up children, plus a crazy moggie.

I love them all dearly, and this wedding jinx wouldn't matter one iota if I was marrying some wild extrovert, someone as nutty as the rest of us. But Huw isn't like that at all.

He's the strong, silent type, reserved in company, easily embarrassed and, if our wedding is another Loveday fiasco, I know he'll hate it. It's not as if Huw's had time to acclimatise himself to the family, either. He met them for the first time only last night. I've tried to give him some inkling of what he's up against – to prepare him, if I could.

I mean, even the way my parents met was unusual. My mother drove her motorbike round a sharp bend one day, skidded on some black ice, and crashed into the cherry tree outside my father's family home. Thrown from the motorbike, she landed at my father's feet. I giggled as I explained it to Huw. 'Father tells everyone that Mother threw herself at him.'

'But, darling, I think that's rather romantic,' Huw said.

'It gets worse,' I warned. 'They named me Cherry after that tree, and called my sisters Rowan and Willow, for good measure.'

Chuckling, Huw insisted, 'They're delightful names.'

'Yes,' I agreed, adding with a touch of light-hearted sarcasm, 'Rowan thought so too, until she married David Tree!'

Laughing, Huw caught me round the waist. 'Lucky for you then, Cherry, that my surname is Jones and not Blossom!'

But nothing I said could really prepare Huw for my family. So the night before he arrived I begged them to go easy on him. Did they listen? Did they do as I'd asked? No chance. After the introductions were made, my brother, Glenn, slapped Huw on the back and chortled, 'Hope the family jinx doesn't strike tomorrow. You'll never guess what happened at my wedding.'

I tried to intervene, but my protests were swamped amid the general hubbub of family hilarity. Glenn put a hand on Huw's shoulder. 'As I reached the church, the heavens opened. Never seen rain like it in my whole life. So I thought, I'll run for it, straight across the churchyard. But I couldn't see a blessed thing.....'

He paused for breath and father finished it for him. 'The silly idiot fell head first into a newly dug grave! You should have seen him, Huw. He was plastered in mud from head to toe.'

Gasping with mirth, Glenn continued, 'Had to rush home, shower and change.'

When the laughter subsided, Huw said in his quiet way, 'Don't worry, I'll make sure I walk on the path.'

But once the family started on the reminiscences, there was no stopping them. In the end, I had to get him to safety. 'Huw's had a long journey,' I pointed out, 'and he needs some rest before tomorrow.' An aunt had offered to put him up in her spare room, and I insisted on driving him there that minute.

Father winked at Huw. 'Dreadful fusspot, our Cherry. Always been the same. Thinks you need protecting from us lot...'

Glenn butted in, 'She warned us, you know.' I'd picked up a little of Huw's lilting Welsh accent, and Glenn began mimicking me in a high-pitched voice. 'Be on your best behaviour with my Huw.' They all jumped in then, trying to outdo each other's Welsh accents.

'Every week, on the phone, she was. Wa-a-nin' us....'

'You'll fr-i-ghten my Huw off....'

'Dead wo-orried, she was, Huw......'

It was impossible to keep a straight face. Huw just stood there grinning in amusement. Huw has a kind and gentle nature, a quiet dignity, an inner strength. His has been a rather solitary life on the family farm. An only child, he took over the farm at 18 when his widowed father died. Even his hobbies are rather solitary. Fishing, walking in his beloved Welsh mountains, and carving animal heads on walking sticks. The most gregarious he gets is taking part in sheepdog trials.

That was how we met – at a sheepdog trial, a few weeks after I moved to Wales. I've always loved watching working sheepdogs and was used to them, having spent a good deal of time on my grandparents' farm.

I'd moved to Wales when the large company I work for closed the office in Newcastle. Some of us were offered transfers and I looked upon the whole thing as an adventure. I am probably the quietest member of the Lovedays, but no-one would ever call me shy. Having watched Huw compete in the trials, I was determined to meet him. I overheard someone say he carved walking sticks to order, and having boldly introduced myself, I placed an order.

'For my father,' I explained, with what I hoped was my most bewitching smile. 'He loves walking.' I was prepared to order walking sticks for each of my three brothers and one brother-in-law, if that's what it took. Luckily, that wasn't necessary, and our relationship galloped along. Despite his reserved manner, Huw knew what he wanted, and that included marriage.

We began making plans for an Easter wedding, sitting cuddled up on the sofa in front of a blazing farmhouse fire. As I snuggled comfortably into the crook of his arm, Huw suddenly blurted out in horror, 'Oh, Lord, I'll have to make a speech at the reception, won't I?' He ran his free hand agitatedly through his hair. 'I'm useless at that sort of thing.'

I started to reassure him when I remembered the family wedding jinx. If only, I thought, I could ensure a perfect day for Huw. No embarrassments, and no disasters. Suddenly I saw the obvious answer. One which meant no speeches either. 'Let's get married quietly,' I urged. 'Here in Wales.'

'We can't do that,' he declared, aghast. 'Think how hurt your parents would be.'

He hadn't met them, or any of my family, as it wasn't easy for him to leave the farm, but he knew what they all meant to me. That was the moment I took a deep breath and told him that if he wanted a proper Loveday wedding, then he ought to know about the wedding jinx.

'Jinx?' he teased. 'Cherry, you don't believe in that sort of thing, surely?'

I looked him straight in the eye. 'Oh, don't I? At Rowan's wedding,' I said, 'the vicar got his dates mixed up and had to be fetched from a cricket match.'

Huw laughed. 'Could happen to anyone, that.'

'At my brother Drummond's wedding,' I continued inexorably, 'my deaf great-aunt, aged 92, suddenly announced, very loudly, in the church, 'The bride's mother looks a right miserable old cow. And you know what they say --- like mother, like daughter.' By the time I'd told him of Glenn's run-in with the grave, Huw had gone very silent. 'I'm the fourth to marry in our family,' I said. 'Don't you see, the jinx is getting worse each time? Honestly, Huw, I'd understand if you'd rather get married here in Wales.'

I curled my arms round his neck and ran my fingers through his dark, wavy hair. 'I want you to have happy memories of our day.'

'Me?' he said in surprise. 'You're worried about me?' I nodded, and he looked deeply into my eyes. 'Do you think, my lovely girl,' he said, 'that I could be happy starting married life without your family there to wish us well?' I hadn't thought of it like that. With tears stinging my eyes, I threw my arms round him, praying that the jinx wouldn't spoil everything.

Huw arranged with a good friend for the farm to be taken care of for ten days to cover the wedding, and our honeymoon in Paris, which is why he didn't arrive in Newcastle until last night.

The wedding is at noon, and it's panic stations in our house. People are rushing everywhere, and everyone wants to get into the bathroom. Nothing changes. Mother leaves her hat on top of the fridge and we find the cat asleep on it. I'd be happy if that was the only thing to go wrong today.

After resuscitating mother's hat, father and I finally dispatch everyone off to the church. Huw phones just before he leaves, and sounds very nervous. And I'm still so jittery father puts his arm round me and assures me everything's going like clockwork. 'Don't you worry, Cherry love, nothing embarrassing will happen at your wedding.'

When we reach the church, I'm almost ready to believe him. Everyone who matters is there. I just catch a glimpse of Huw and the vicar hurrying back towards the vestry. I guess he's forgotten to sign something.

The best man keeps patting the pocket that holds the ring. Mother is in her place, along with every member of our family. The organist sits ready and waiting. And, at last, I relax. Everything is going to be all right, after all.

When the vicar reappears, I know Huw must be close behind, and I turn to father, who smiles. 'Here we go, Cherry.' He takes my arm and whispers, 'Did I tell you how beautiful you look?'

'Thanks, Dad,' I say happily. 'Thanks for everything.'

I take a deep, calming breath and wait for the organist to begin. But nothing happens. I check my bouquet, the bridesmaids smooth their dresses. Still no music. The organist exchanges glances with the vicar, who just shrugs. I look down the aisle and my heart begins to pound. Huw isn't there.

No Loveday has ever been jilted at the altar. Surely he hasn't – not Huw. Then I recall how nervous he'd sounded on the phone. Perhaps he'd wanted to tell me then and hadn't been able to. Then I hear a strange, muffled hammering noise.

The vicar goes off to investigate and the congregation begins whispering again. The hammering grows louder and more insistent, and so does my heart. Father says, 'Stay here, Cherry love. I'll find out what's going on.' I try to beg him not to leave me, but my tongue is stuck fast to the roof of my mouth.

Five long minutes pass before he appears again. He speaks briefly to the best man, then standing in front of the guests, he announces with all his usual jollity, 'Does anyone have a screwdriver? The bridegroom's locked in the loo!'

Huw hasn't run out on me. The family jinx has struck again. Needless to say, the whole congregation erupts with laughter. The Lovedays' reputation is intact. Father goes on, 'The lock has broken and we need a screwdriver to take the door hinges off.'

A guest gets one from his car, but by the time the service eventually begins, people are arriving for the next wedding. It's utter chaos --- in typical Loveday style --- but all I can think of is Huw and how desperately embarrassed he must be.

When I finally reach his side, I look up in trepidation, to find his eyes are glowing with love, not embarrassment. In that brief moment, I realise how wrong I've been.

Wrong to imagine that his reserved manner and solitary lifestyle would prevent him coping with a mere jinx. Wrong to believe that a man who's run a farm from the age of eighteen, isn't used to overcoming problems. Huw's never needed me to protect him. I'm a fool not to have realised that before.

Grinning hugely at me, Huw winks, 'Guess I'm really one of the family now!'

THE END

OTHER TITLES BY DAWN HARRIS
All available from Amazon
Novels:----
The Drusilla Davanish mystery thriller series

Letter From A Dead Man

The Fat Badger Society

The Ebenezer Papers (1930s mystery thriller)

Collection of short stories

Dinosaur Island

Reviews for "Letter From A Dead Man."

"A delightful murder mystery in an 18th century setting." Historical Novel Society

"Letter From A Dead Man has a similar wit to Pride and Prejudice, and Harris holds up a mirror to society in the sort of way that Austen did." Margot Kinberg, whose Confessions of a Mystery Novelist have brought her many awards in America.

Reviews for "The Fat Badger Society."

"The book sits well within the historical mystery genre, and I have no hesitation in recommending The Fat Badger Society as an enjoyable historical read." Historical Novel Society.

"This story has everything: excitement, mystery, humour and romance. Great stuff!" Sheila Norton, popular award winning author.

Printed in Great Britain
by Amazon